# *The Lies Hustlers Never Tell*

A Nu Direction Publishing
A division of
MeJah Books Incorporated

Note:
This book is a work of fiction. Names, characters, places and incidents are products of the author's imagination or are used fictitiously. Any resemblance to actual events or locales or persons, living or dead, is entirely coincidental.

Published by A Nu Direction Publishing
a division of MeJah Books Incorporated
MeJah Books
Tri-State Mall #12-13
333 Naamans Road
Claymont, DE 19703

ISBN: 09765733-0-X
Copyright:2004

The Lies Hustlers Never Tell
Story by Shahida Fennell
Editing & Text formation by Janus Bryant & Megan Karchner
Consulting by Azarel Life Changing Books, Inc.
Cover by OCJ GRAPHIX
Cover photography by APS Photo
Printed by RR Donnelley

# *The Lies Hustlers Never Tell*

*by*

## *Shahida T. Fennell*

A Note From The Author:

This book is not about a particular person nor is it meant to offend anyone in or out of the game. There is a flip side to every coin and this book is touching my point of view based on my experience, which became The Lies Hustlers Never Tell. I'm not glorifying the game in any way, but the reality is there are only three things that can come out of the game: If you escape death, there's always jail-- if you miss that, you usually become the nigga you use to serve. So if the shoe don't fit, don't wear it!! Just enjoy the story because I'm sure you have heard or seen or know someone who fits these characteristics. So sit back and enjoy 'cause don't you think the lies need to be uncovered?!

## STOP THE VIOLENCE

As a people we have lost too many to so much. I have dedicated my life to Aids Research and as I promote abstinence I also live in the real world. Practice Safe Sex.

## THE LIES HUSTLERS NEVER TELL

The lies a hustler never tell
Takin' welfare checks to flip
Getting rentals in my name, so you can floss with those other chicks
Using me as your sperm deposit
While skeletons fill up your closet
Wearing your name as a bracelet-- PROUD
While tattooed asses, arms and tits
Got your head filled with gas, when it should be filled with shame
Those chicks don't even know your government name
SO YOU LAUGH
Not that you're glad Naaah!
You need somewhere for your dope to be stashed
So you play a half-ass dad, claiming only some
Those chicks don't know that you're an undercover bum
Got fat pockets, iced out and flashy cars
If they only knew who you really ARE
Driving your BMW in your baby momma's name
To keep it on the low you pay her
Flossing in your ice--an imaginary player
You stay in something fly,
Truth be told one of your girls is a booster
Your life is filled with lies, tricks, deceit and fantasy
See the lies a hustler never tell
Will haunt him and be his worst enemy.

Shahida T. Fennell

# Dedication

THIS BOOK COULD NOT BE DEDICATED TO
ONE PERSON SO I have dedicated it to the
three most important women in my life.

She carried me six months
So I knew all her inner thoughts
We shared laughter, and tears
Month after month
I learned things that could only be taught by her
Embraced with the good and bad she showed me the ups and the downs
She made sure I had this world somewhat figured out
Time after time I wondered why she was in such a rush
She was preparing me for life
You know - life after her
Not yet understanding just taking mental notes
Forever together
At least that's what I had hoped
As time passed and the hour struck
I thanked God for you but our time was up
So now I know why you rushed and taught me so much
You only get one mother and mine was the best

April Yvette Fennell 11/02/58 TO 09/05/94

God Mom — Throughout the struggle someone has to help maintain balance;
you gave me encouragement the days I was down, you held me up the days I
wanted to fall and when everyone walked out you made it happen just on the
strength. You have been more than a mother.
LOVE YOU Ms. Emlyn. DeGannes

God Mom — My mother passed away and you were her only true friend.
You kept your word and upheld your position and the deepest part is you are
there for both her children. LOVE YOU Barbara Henson.

**I was once told by a somewhat wise man that "nothing in life is constant
but change" so with that I also dedicate this book to all the single mothers who are holding things down by themselves. Anyone can make a baby
but it takes a hell of a man to raise one.**

*Extra special thanks to:*
*Lee-Mudd much success in your life's career*


## Special thanks
*Pastor Derrick Johnson*
*Michelle Anderson*
*Janus Bryant*
*Megan A. Karchner*
*Carmen Perkins*
*Hope Rose (Photographer)*
*Vince Seaton*
*Shaylynn Wallace*

*Keisha, Samira, Stacey and Nikki have more in common than they think. They love the same man and they play different roles in his world. He's the Don Juan of the city; the player of all players to some, but these women know the lies he never tells. See, in the world of a hustler, things may seem all gravy but the truth be told, everything that shine ain't gold. Things are never what they really seem, so let the truth unfold...*

# CHAPTER 1

## A Mirage

Every morning for the past week, Nikki had been in the bathroom. *What the hell is wrong with me? God please, don't let me be pregnant. I've only been with this guy for four months and barely know him. DAMN, I don't even know his government name! I haven't finished school yet; I'm just a junior. My parents will go berserk!*

Nikki's thoughts raced as she hovered over the toilet, careful not to be too loud because her father had just come out of his room. There was a loud knock on the bathroom door. "Nikki," called her father, "Are you okay?"

"Yes daddy, I'm fine. My stomach hurts a little."

Nikki got up, washed and dressed. She put on her VonDutch jeans with a tee-shirt and matching baseball cap. She didn't feel like curling her hair. Simone was meeting her at Rite Aid in a few minutes and she had to walk. She dared not tell her father that Ace had her car. "Love you dad!" Nikki screamed as she rushed out the door, so he wouldn't ask any more questions.

Simone was at Rite Aid on time as usual. She was steaming because Nikki was a little late and she had every intention on telling her about herself. "Shut the hell up!" said Nikki, finally showing up with an attitude. "I don't want to hear it! My dad was being nosy, so I had to be careful how I came out the house."

Simone answered in a smart way, "Look here, I'm not gonna be doin' this shit every day!" Nikki quickly snapped, "What! How the hell are you gonna' to act like that? You know that Ace looks out and as my friend, you will do this for me!"

They drove down Market Street saying very little to each other, towards the Eastside- Clifford Brown Walk, where Simone lived. As they pulled up in front of the house, Nikki called Ace, but his voice mail picked up on the first ring. Pissed, but trying not to show Simone her emotions, she tried his phone again. She thought to herself, damn this nigga knows I have to go to work in a half hour. Where the hell is he?

Simone could see her friend was feeling some kind of way about Ace. She didn't want to be the one to hate on their relationship, but Simone concluded that nigga Ace ain't shit.

As they entered Simone's house, Nikki ran directly to the bathroom and began to throw up. She took so long in the there, Simone got curious. "Yo Nikki what's wrong? I hope your ass ain't pregnant!"

"Hmm, I hope not," Simone responded fearing the worst.

She has too much going for her to get caught up in that nigga Ace's shit. Nikki was a junior in college and worked at Neiman Marcus part-time to help put herself through school. She still lived at home with her parents in a comfortable home and she was her parents' only child. Her dad was an OB/GYN; her mother, a school teacher. She had a beautifully voluptuous figure with a cute baby face and now…Simone's thoughts trailed off, interrupted by the sound of her friend puking her guts out.

Hooooooonk! A horn blew outside on the busy block.

"NIKKI!" Ace yelled from over the boomin' system of Nikki's Lexus SUV.

"Hey nigga, pull over!" yelled a guy stopped behind Ace in a Crown Victoria..

"Nigga, wait a minute, you don't have no place to go!" screamed Ace.

"Who that?" asked the guy in the Crown Vic', getting angry before noticing it was Ace.

"Oh-it's my man Ace from the Villa! You goin' to the game

2

tonight?" he asked.

"Of course!" Ace confirmed.

They held a brief conversation from one car to the next until Ace grew impatient.

"Nikki!" he screamed at the top of his lungs. Hooonk!

Even though they had been dating for only four months, Nikki was head over heels for Ace. They met at Club 2000, on a Friday night at a comedy show. She could see he liked to show off, he had sent her and her friends drinks all night. See, Ace was a charmer. He knew how to get whatever and whomever he wanted.

The first weekend they met, he spent major money-flying her to Vegas first-class with limousine service to and from the airport which included a tour of the strip. They were treated like royalty at the luxurious Venetian Hotel, VIP accommodations all the way and it was as if he had money to burn. There were all day shopping sprees from the Forum shops at Caesar's, to the Fremont Experience, to the Fashion Show mall. And every meal was eaten at some of the most exclusive restaurants in Vegas. They pulled the slots everywhere and they even took in a couple of shows like the Untamed Tongues Poetry Lounge held at the refreshingly upscale, Sweet Georgia Browns. All this impressed Nikki. She had been spoiled all her life, so for this man to spoil her more, overwhelmed her with joy. He was just too good to be true. She was uplifted by the thought of their beginning.

She also thought about the fact that he never talked about neither his family nor his personal life. She sort of liked the mysterious part of him though. Plus, all the other guys she used to date weren't as nearly as exciting.

She had been a little sheltered growing up, but Ace lived on the edge, and she loved it! Their first thirty days together was like gravy. Ace took her to so many places. They went to dinner every Friday night. Nikki especially liked to go to Philly to her favorite place, Tangerines, a nice little jazzy spot in Center City.

"Hey babe, why did it take you so long to come outside? You got me holdin' up traffic and stuff," said Ace when Nikki came out of the house. "How's my baby today?" he asked, charming her as she walked towards him. Her face was pale and she looked exhausted.

"Damn!" screamed Ace, as she got closer to the car and he got a good look at her. "So what took you so long, and why do you look like that?"

"I spent the morning in the bathroom. I'm not feeling too good Ace," replied Nikki, looking drained. "I don't think I'm going to work today. I just want to go home and get some rest. How come when I called your phone this morning, it went straight to voice-mail on the first ring?" Nikki asked in a soft but firm tone. "Babe, I thought we already discussed you being available for me at all times, like you were when we first met," Nikki explained trying not to get angry by the smirk on Ace's face. "What is more important than me?" she whined.

"Well, I had to go to a parent-teacher conference this morning and I left my phone in the car," Ace reassured her.

"Yeah? That's what's up," said Nikki, satisfied with his explanation.

One of the reasons she believed he was the man of her dreams in the first place, was because aside from being very good to her, he was a great father to his son, unlike too many black men in the streets that she had encountered.

"It's been four months, when am I going to meet your son?" asked Nikki since he had brought up the subject.

"Babe, I told you soon," he voiced, but what he really felt was, yeah right, never! I don't let just anyone meet him. He's my pride and joy, not to mention my only child. His heart softened with the mere thought of his son.

"How old is he again?" Nikki pressed.

4

"He's ten, and that's enough about my son," he said short-ly. Then he quickly changed the subject. "Where are you goin' because I need to handle some business, so I can pay for your next semester of school?"

"I told you my tuition was already paid, sweetie, but what you can do is make some money so I can go to Cancun with Simone," Nikki replied as quickly as he had changed the subject.

"All right babe," Ace said giving her that one. "I'm gonna' drop you off at home. Chirp me later once you feel better."

They approached her parent's home and Nikki checked around to make sure they had already left for work. As she scoped out the block, she played things off by making small talk with Ace. "Babe, so how long are you going to be?"

"I'll only be a little while," Ace said. "You just need to get some rest, and later we'll catch a movie."

"OK," she agreed, satisfied the coast was clear. "Love you Ace." Nikki blushed. "Love you back," he replied.

Ace laid back in the fully-loaded Lexus blasting Jay-Z, "*...if you're havin' girl problems/ I feel bad for you son/ I got ninety-nine problems but a bitch ain't one...!*" Ace felt his phone vibrating, so he turned the music down just a little bit to answer, "YO!"

"Yeah nigga, it's me. Your son needs a pair of Rocawear sneakers!" a female voice spit from the other end.

"Man look, Rocawear don't make sneakers, stupid," Ace laughed to keep from getting angry.

"Nigga you know what I mean, and bring some milk and Pampers for Aceisha," demanded the young girl.

"Yo, didn't I say I wanna' get a blood test for that little girl?" Ace insisted.

"Fuck you nigga!" the girl went off. "Every time I want somethin' from you for your daughter, you always wanna' holla' about some damn blood test! And you still wanna' be

5

sleepin' wit' me and shit, you nasty bastard? I bet that Muslim bit...."

"YO! What did I tell you about that disrespectful shit?" Ace cut in, his temper pretty warmed up. "Didn't I tell you to never mention my girl? Just for talkin' stupid, I ain't buyin' shit!
Don't fuckin' call me no more you dumb bitch!"

"Mother Fucker!!! I don't even know that girl's name! Fuck you and her!!!! I saw you rollin' around in that Lexus like you da' shit when your kids need sneaks. You bastard!" she screamed hysterically.

"Take me to court, bitch!" yelled Ace, and he banged on her.

*"...I got ninety-nine problems but a bitch ain't one...!"* Jay-Z proudly declared from the twelve-speaker sound system of Nikki's plush midnight blue Lex' SUV. Wishing he could say the same thing, Ace hit the highway-north on 95, up top to Philly.

*He never told you about the two baby moms*
*No job, no crib, three or four kids*
*And car ain't his*
*Shit's a mirage*
*He dodgin' child support*
*But you think its bullets*
*No license, but he pushin' your whip*
*The life of a hustler or should I say wankster*
*TV's the only place where*
*That nigga seen gangsta'*
*It's a desert*
*No water*
*But you see a stream*
*Damn its crazy the things*
*You see in a dream...*

## A MIRAGE

# CHAPTER 2

## Bloody Money

*It's gonna be mad chicks at this game tonight*, Ace thought smiling, as he blazed on the highway jamming to the music. This was going to be the game of the winter, and it was being battled out at Howard High: Howard vs. Glasgow. Howard had the young boy, Hashim, Ace's childhood friend and Muslim brother from the East-side. And Glasgow had the boy Aaron aka Pearl. They both had game, so there was gonna be major war both on and off the court. Ace had 5G's on Howard, all on the strength of Hashim's skills, Ace reminded himself as he approached his exit off 76-West.

He parked in the *no-park zone* smack in front of Dr. Denim on South Street. He hopped out of the car and ran in the store to get an outfit for the game. Never shying away from an opportunity to shine, he pulled out his hustler knot, after he placed his stuff on the counter. The young lady behind the desk could see he was really working as she rang up, folded and bagged his purchase. She smiled and said, "That will be two hundred seventy-five dollars." He gave her three crisp one hundred dollar bills and told her to keep the change. He knew he would be in the store again and that she would definitely remember him, so he didn't even bother to ask her name.

He dropped the bags back at the car and went to Ishka-bibbles to order a cheese-steak. After all, how can I come to Philly and not get a steak Philly-style? Ace reasoned, mouth watering with anticipation of the first bite. While waiting for hisfood, he ran two stores down to Unica and got his son two pair of Air One's

9

with Rocawear sweat suits to match. He went back, picked up his steak, hopped into Nikki's Lex' and peeled off to 95-South back to Delaware, shocked as hell he hadn't gotten a parking ticket this time.

Licking the last of the ketchup off his fingers, Ace tossed his cheese-steak wrapper out the window totally satisfied; then he got on the phone and called his boy Rick. Rick and Ace were like brothers. They had been friends since they were five years old.

"Yo! Rick where you at?" he hollered into his speaker phone.

"Who's this, Ali?" Rick laughed through the speaker.

Perturbed, Ace said, "What did I tell you about callin' out my government name on these government phones? You the only nigga I allow to call me that. Damn Rick! Anyway, I need for you to go to Keisha's house and start baggin' up that dope for the night rush; before you go pick up some Pampers and milk for her daughter," Rick laughed.

"Look nigga, I am not your errand boy, but I know we gotta' get money so I'll do it."

"Aww nigga you always complainin'. For once, just do what I asked," said Ace.

"Alright," said Rick, "One."

As Ace continued south towards Wilmington, he turned the music up, just in time to catch his boy, 50 Cents. *"...I don't know what you heard about me/but a bitch can't get a dollar out of me/no Cadillac, no perms you can't see/that I'm a motherfucking P-I-M-P..."* While he listened to the music, he drifted up into his head to plot his next move. He also thought about Samira and their growing up together. From the moment he saw her beautiful caramel complexion, long silky hair and long lean body, he knew it was love. *"...girl we could pop some champagne and we could have a ball/we could toast to the good life, girl we could have it all/we could really splurge girl, and tear up the mall/if ever you needed someone, I'm the one you should call..."*

His thoughts began to flip-flop between Samira and the game; and it was not only overwhelming him, but also giving him a headache. *"...I'm a motherfucking P-I-M-P..."* This nigga ain't never lied, he thought as he tuned back into his song and grooved all the way home.

Back in Wilmington, as Ace approached the Martin Luther King exit to Fourth Street, he came down off the cloud he was riding on, from the vibration of his cell phone. It was his son, little Ali.

"As Salaam Alaikum, Abbe. Peace be unto you, Dad!" he greeted with all his ten year old exuberance.

"Wa Lakum Salaam son. What are you doin'?" asked Ace, beaming at the sound of his boy's voice.

"Nothin'," said little Ali. "I want to go bowling this weekend Abbe. Can we go?"

"Inshallah son, God willing. Where's your mom?" asked Ace.

"She's asleep," Ali said, "I'll tell her you asked for her later. Call me later, Abbe."

Just as he was hanging up the phone from his son, Keisha called. Instead of answering her call, he pushed the 'no' button, and she went straight to voice-mail. He saw there were messages, but decided to check them later. He forgot which code he was using; since the phone was in Samira's name, he often changed his code. I'll have to try them all later, he decided as he cruised through West-side before heading home. As quiet as it was kept, he lived with his mother in a row house on Heald Street, in back of Kentucky Fried Chicken.

Ace, born Ali Prince, was the baby of three children. He had two older sisters, who were grown and out the house. Ace parked the car in the backyard driveway, and headed in the house. Before he turned the doorknob to go in, he turned off his cell phone. He had way too much respect for his mom to involve her in anything he did in the streets, including his phone ringing non-stop. Hearing him coming up the outside steps, his mother inquired, "Ali whose car is that parked in my driveway?"

*Damn-she don't miss nothin'*, he thought. "It's my friend's car," he politely answered as he rushed upstairs.

He dropped his clothes in his room, then jumped in the shower. The steamy hot water felt so good to him, that he could clearly focus on all the money to be made. Feeling fresh and clean, he stepped out of the shower, quickly dried off and put on some ball shorts and a tee. He wanted to chill and shoot the breeze with his mom for a while since he hadn't seen her in two days.

Ali was spoiled, and as twisted as it was, that's what made him start hustlin'. His mother had struggled throughout all the years of raising the girls, but by the time Ali was born, she was financially established, so he hustled mainly for kicks not because he needed to.

Ali's dad died before he was born. He was murdered in a botched robbery. And time after time, his sisters never let him forget how much he acted and looked just like their father.

"Mom," said Ace, "has anyone called me?"

"No, Ace, Samira hasn't called," his mother gently replied. Mrs. Prince knew that Samira had been the only woman who had called there for him in the past twelve years. Samira had been with him when he had nothing and she also knew the real him. She could care less about his flash or ruthless reputation and that was why he loved her so much.

Sensing Ace's disappointment, his mother tried to cheer him up, "But little Ali called last night to tell me about his grades."

"Yeah, I know," smiled Ace, "I had a meeting this morning at his school, he's doing really well. Samira is a good mother.

She reminds me of you Ma," Ace trailed as he began to walk out of his mother's room.

"Oh yeah Mom, may I use your VISA? I need a rental to take little Ali bowling this weekend."

"Look boy," his mom scolded, "I'll do it this time, but how many times are you going to need rentals? This is the fifth one this month. Money doesn't grow on trees. You need to get a job and get out of those streets."

*Pryin' into my business again,* Ace thought. "…and whose car is that in my driveway again?"

Ace pretended he didn't hear his mother and shut the bedroom door quietly, in the middle of her ranting.

***

Nikki awakened to the ringing of the phone.

"Hey girl, get up!" screamed Simone in her ear. "You know it's a game tonight at Howard. How are you feelin'? What was wrong anyway?"

Nikki avoided the questions. "So what, there's a game! I don't even have anything to wear. Let me call you right back, anyway. I want to see where the hell Ace is so we can go to the mall."

Nikki hung up with Simone and dialed Ace. Once again, his voice-mail picked up on the first ring. "It's me babe, I'm feelin' better. Give me a call. I need my car," she said, leaving yet another message.

Stretching across his plush king-size bed, Ace began to count his money. He only had a thousand dollars to start with and he had already spent three hundred on himself and three hundred on his son. *Damn I'm down to only four hundred dollars left,* Ace thought. He dozed off, after a long day of running the streets.

***

13

Nikki was frustrated because she had not been able to contact Ace for the past two hours. She hadn't seen him since that morning and she tried to convince herself that he must have been doing something important like spending quality time with his son. He sure as hell wasn't checking for her like he said he would. Disgusted, Nikki called Simone. "Hey girl maybe you can come get me and we can go to the mall before the game."

"Ok girl," agreed Simone. "Meet me at Rite Aid in five minutes."

Nikki got up and brushed her teeth, feeling crazy about not hearing from Ace. She then ran downstairs, but before leaving the house, she grabbed a handful of grapes and a bottle of juice from the 'fridge. She left the house and walked to Rite Aid to meet Simone. Once they hooked up, off to the mall they went.

*** 

Ace rose to the aroma of food. His mother had cooked him dinner, like always. She babied him by leaving his plate in the microwave every night, even nights he didn't come home. He followed his nose to the kitchen where he retrieved his plate and sat at the dining room table to eat. His thoughts of Samira kept him company. He knew she wouldn't continue to go for his bullshit so he picked up the cordless phone and called her.

"As Salaam Alaikum," Ace greeted Samira.

"Wa Lakum Salaam," she returned. "Hold on let me get little Ali…"

"Wait, wait," Ace called, "I wanted to speak to you."

"*What*?" Samira paused suspiciously.

"I miss you. Can you go bowling with me and little Ali this weekend?"

"No," said Samira flatly without hesitation. "I'm not confusing my son by having him think we're going to be a family.

Plus, I have plans, since he'll be with you."

"I picked up two pair of sneakers and sweats to match for him," said Ace, hoping that would soften her.

"That's nice," said Samira unimpressed. She played the role of strength, but deep inside she really loved Ace.

He was the only man she had ever been with, but he had also hurt her too many times. She resigned herself to the fact that the streets had him now, and she refused to be caught up in his bullshit.

"Look Ali, I have go. I'm about to cook," she said.

"Yo Samira," Ace interrupted. "I love you, man. Why can't you just believe that? I'm going crazy without you and our son."

Samira heard the pain in Ali's voice. "Every time you kick that love stuff, I pray that it's true but you need to show me. You haven't changed anything. You still run the streets and mess with all those different girls. I don't need that in my life," her voice cracked.

Attempting to pull herself together, she went on. "Ok Ali, enough of this love talk. Call me back later. Maybe I'll go bowling with you and Ali this weekend. And don't forget to pay the mortgage, it was due yesterday," she reminded him.

"Alright," said Ace sadly. "I love you Samira. Please just think of giving me a chance."

"I'll see, Salaam Alaikum," she barely uttered and hung up.

After hanging up with Samira, Ace put his dishes in the sink and got dressed. He got his cell phone, locked up the house, and hopped into Nikki's Lexus heading to the East-side to pick up his money from Kedar and Black; a few cats that hustled for him.

Kedar was a little, fat, light-skinned guy. He was a ladies man who always played way too much.

"Kedar, what up? You got that?" asked Ace.

Smiling, Kedar said, "Man, I only have two-fifty for you."

"What?" asked Ace, in a don't-play-with-me tone. "Look, you got 'til midnight to come up with that cash. I'll have Rick pick that up later."

"Peace," said Kedar. "I got you." As Kedar gave Ace the money he did have, Ace yanked him into the window of the SUV.

"Take things more seriously. You never know when the joke will be on you," Ace said seriously.

He roughly let him go, smirked and pulled off. Kedar knew he had to have Ace's money. Ace wasn't the type to play games when it came to his money.

\*\*\*

Just a couple blocks away, Ace realized his phone was off and turned it on. He had twelve messages. In the background Mario Winans pleaded for the ladies to keep the games on the low 'cause his heart couldn't take it anymore.

"Yo Ace!" Hashim's voice called from the speaker of his Nextel. "Pick up your tickets for the game from my mom's."

"Yo, make sure you do your thing tonight. I got a lotta money ridin' on you Haji," Ace coached.

"Man you know me. I'm like Lebron James on these cats. They can't hold me!" Hashim laughed confidently.

"Alright. One," said Ace. Before he could put his phone down, Nikki called finally getting through.

"Hey babe," said Ace.

"Hey babe." Nikki snapped, "Where the hell are you?"

"Around," said Ace. "I'm still takin' care of business and you better be in the house when I come by to pick you up. I'll be there soon."

"Later," Nikki complied. She never told him that she was already at the mall and would be at the game whether she went with him or not.

The next stop was the projects to see if Rick took care of things for Keisha.

"Yo Keisha!" Ace hollered as he opened the door with his key to the dusty project house.

"Yeah, yeah," Keisha responded. "Did you get my message? I sent Rick to drop off work and also Pampers and milk for the baby. Clean this fuckin' house up," he added unnecessarily.

Ace regarded Keisha as a real smut, but she held all his drugs and did a lot of his street business for him.

"Rick just left," said Keisha. "And I'm sorry for bein' such a bitch earlier." She whispered in his ear, "I wanna' see you tonight so I can give you some of this good stuff."

Unmoved, Ace said, "Yo Keisha, why you all dressed up? Weave nice and done up. Where you goin'?"

"To the game," Keisha responded, secretly hurt by his rejection.

"Be back by eleven," Ace reprimanded. "We got business tonight."

"Alright! I need some money." Keisha informed him.

"What? Be in by eleven or else," Ace threatened, totally ignoring her financial request.

"I heard you," Keisha replied. She knew not to get smart with him in person.

17

*Shahida T. Fennell*

*Bloody Money*
*See it's funny*
*It's funny how blood oozes off this money*
*This money sure is bloody*
*I got nicks, he got twenties and the cat around back got*
*weight*
*But wait*
*You won't escape the rape of these streets*
*'Cause the minute you peep, I got you*
*There goes nigga noddin', black on black robbin' junkies*
*Slobberin'*
*Middle fingers in the air saying fuck the police drivin'*
*That's how money got me*
*Bloody*
*Bloody Money, Bloody Money*

*Small faces, big faces, pennies and nickels and dimes*
*It all gets chased; I want it all to be mine*
*From bakin' up fake cake to flip as weight*
*To layin' a cat flat on his back ready for blood*
*Splat*
*To spendin' cash for ass hollerin' at a hood rat*
*That's how money got me*
*Bloody*
*Blood Money, Bloody Money*

*Girls cryin' they say my little brother died*
*Ghost visits, no lawyer for trial*
*Collect calls rejected, appeal denied*
*My mans got my spot on the block*
*And my main bitch on lock*
*As diamonds flood my Jacob watch*
*The time stops... whoever said the game was fair*
*Bloody*
*Blood Money, Bloody Money*

**Blood Money**

"Yo, I'm out front," he chirped through his Nextel walkie-talkie phone. Ace spoke, before turning it to vibrate. As soon as Rick got in the car, they talked about Kedar; Ace let Rick know that he wanted him to collect money from Kedar that night after the game. Rick happily agreed because he and Kedar had beef over Hashim's sister, Nadirah before and he was going to love every minute of getting the money from him.

***

Nikki got ready for the evening at Simone's house; she put on her dark blue Polo jean set with the new Gucci sneaks Ace had gotten her while they were in Vegas. And of course, there was a Gucci bag to match. Before leaving, Nikki tried to call Ace one more time, but the phone just rang and rang. Leaving a message, "It's me again; I guess you're tied up with something real important. You didn't even ask if I needed my car, so I'm going to the game with Simone. I'll call you later."

# CHAPTER 3

## Fake Ass Ballin' Bitch

When Simone and Nikki entered the game, it seemed as though the whole city was there. Everybody from the ballers to the stick-up kids and the queens to the smuts. It was definitely packed.

Starting number 44, point guard, Hashim 'Haji' Fennell, had just caught a no-look pass and broke Pearl's ankles with the killa' crossover. He hit the fade-away, three pointer right in his mouth!

The crowd was going crazy and that was exactly why there were mad scouts at the game praying that theirs was the school that Haji chose. Amidst all the excitement, Simone spotted Terrence whom she knew had the hots for Nikki. She also knew that Ace and Terrence weren't cool either, but she hated to see her friend feeling down over Ace. She grabbed a couple of seats next to him and his boys.

"What's up, Terrence! Let Nikki sit next to you! I'll sit behind y'all so I can see better." That was fine with Terrence. He smiled from ear-to-ear. He wanted to hit that so bad.

Ace and Rick were so into the game, they hadn't noticed Keisha and her ghetto crew walking in all loud and ready to start trouble. Not to mention, the distraction of everybody walking by, giving them dap.

As Ace turned to speak to Pearl's brothers, Ju and Kyle, he noticed Nikki on the bleachers sitting next to Terrence. Rick noticed Ace's complexion go from beige to red.

"Yo, Ace, what's wrong?"

21

Ace, blinded by rage, did not respond; he just started walking towards the bleachers and Rick followed.

Neither of them even noticed that the crowd had gotten real hyped when Shakir stole the ball from Hashim. He dunked on him with nothin' but hang time, his braids spraying a shower of sweat in Haji's face! Ace paid none of this any attention. He was too focused on Nikki, who smiled as Terrence whispered something to her.

With one swift motion, he pushed Simone out of the way and yanked Nikki up by her ponytail, pushing her aside to be dealt with later. Meanwhile, Keisha who was the type to fight any and every female Ace openly messed with, sat on the other side of the bleachers and watched the whole scene unfold.

Before Terrence could react, Ace slapped him with the butt of his .38 revolver. Blood flew everywhere as Rick cocked his fist back ready to release a blow to the guy sitting next to Terrence. With Terrence out the way, Ace grabbed Nikki by the arm and advanced towards the door, oblivious to the scattering crowd, including Keisha and her friends who followed Ace to witness the beat down.

In the parking lot he gripped her tightly, close to him, and breathed fire.

"Yo, you apparently don't know the rules. You belong to me," he said staring her dead in her eyes. What's mine don't be at no game with a bunch of niggas." Ace's usually soft, boyish face was now as hard as stone. The look in his eyes was sinister.

"Ace, you're hurting my arms," cried Nikki, trying not to attract any more attention.

"Get in the car!" Ace growled.

As Nikki bolted for her SUV, Keisha slinked up behind Ace. "Ace," she called, "Ace, I know you hear me."

Ignoring Keisha, Ace got in the car and sped to Brandywine where he parked in a dark spot.

Without looking at her, he said, "Look here, don't you ever disrespect me like that again. You know you don't go out in public without letting me know first. Yo, I don't play! You belong to me and don't forget it. I will fuck you up," he said calmly, grabbing her face and forcefully squeezing her cheeks.

"Stop Ace. Stop!" Nikki cried.

"Yo, Ace, where you at?" Rick chirped.

"Man look, meet me at the south spot. One," Ace spat into the receiver. Turning back to Nikki, "Look here, don't ever do that shit again, you hear me?"

"Look, Ace," Nikki whimpered, "I'm going to drop you off so you can be with that girl from the game, then I'm going home."         "WHAT, you still talkin' stupid!" he yelled slapping her. Then he got out the car and started to walk, knowing she would come after him. True to form, she followed him in the car down the dark road, honking the horn and begging for him to get in.

"Ace, wait," pleaded Nikki, "Where are you going? You can't walk from here in the dark. Get in the car, please."

Hearing Nikki grovel, Ace smirked and thought, *I got her.*

"I'm sorry, Ace!" she cried frantically.

He stopped walking and slid into the passenger seat.

"Look Nik, I love you but that was your only chance to get it right. You know I'm a jealous man. Nothing of mine will ever be with anyone else, understand? Now I got beef with this nigga Terrence, not that it's a problem. So peep this. I need you to stay in the house until this shit blows over and if you do go out, I wanna' know every little step you take."

Nikki shook and sobbed silently as she drove to Simone's house, where Ace instructed her to leave her car out front and to have Simone take her home.

"I have to handle some business tonight, so go home. I'll get with you on Sunday 'cause I have my son all day Saturday," he said matter-of-factly, as if he hadn't just smacked her up. As they pulled up, Simone was in the door being nosy as usual.

"Are you okay, girl?" Simone asked running up to the car.

"Why," Ace chimed in. "What if she wasn't okay, what was you gonna do?" Ace smiled, thinking how fat Simone's butt was in those Dolce & Gabbana jeans. Nikki, on the other hand, asked herself why she had gone to the game in the first place.

She thought about how she had started a big mess without even knowing it and how now, Ace had beef with the West-side, all over her.

"I love you Ace," she said apologetically. Turning his back on her, Ace chirped Kedar.

"Meet me on Clifford Brown Walk. I need a ride to the south spot. One."

Then turning back to Nikki, he spoke coolly. "The next nigga's face I see you in, will be the last face either of y'all see." And from what she saw in his eyes, she knew he was telling the truth.

***

At home as usual, Samira, listened as the teachings of the Holy Quran drifted through her living room. She thought about how much little Ali looked like his father and how she really loved Ace. She wanted so badly for him to leave the streets so that they could be a family again. She called Ace's phone and got his voice mail on the first ring. *I should try to check his messages*, she thought. She called again. Samira got his voice-mail once more. Knowing how he felt about little Ali, she wondered if his code was his son's birthday, October, 24th. She pushed in 1-0-2-4 and hit the jackpot on the first try. He had twelve messages.

The first message was from Keisha. "Hey, babe. Thanks for the stuff. Rick brought it through…"

The second message was from a girl named Nikki, talking about she needed her car. *This nigga still ain't shit*, Samira thought. There were five messages total from Keisha, talking stupid as usual, and the rest were from that new babe, Nikki. *I knew about Keisha stashing drugs and doing runs, but why is he still fucking this bitch?* she wondered hurt and disgusted. *Nikki must be a new chick on his squad. These girls are all crazy thinking they have themselves open for him,* she thought. Samira did her best not to get angry because she knew what it was with him, so she decided not to listen to anymore.

The knowledge that he was still in the field doing him, and apparently everybody else, would help her, once she was ready to leave his ass.

***

Kedar had picked up Ace from CB. As they rode through the East-side to get to the Southbridge projects, they listened to Usher's *Let It Burn*.

"What up, Black!" Ace hollered out the window of Kedar's squatter as they cruised. They approached Keisha's place to find Keisha and her girls out front, smoking weed and drinking.

"Yeah Ace, I seen you and your new little bitch at the game. How she get to ride in the Lexus? I told you about bringin' bitches to the 'hood," Keisha laughed as Ace hopped out the black Crown Victoria.

"Yo, I'm not in a good mood, so go somewhere before I fuck you up," Ace growled. "As a matter of fact, tell them stupid bitches they got to go and you get in here. We got business to tend to. Where the kids at?"

"They're with my mother," Keisha barely replied. She was too busy getting turned on, eyeing Ace, who was looking good in his new denim set with crisp, tan Timberland 'butters' on; not to mention his jet black, curly hair was expertly tapered and he smelled like he had just-stepped-out-the-shower.

He sat at the kitchen table, called Kedar over and began to bag the dope. Keisha honestly believed the nastier she was, the more Ace would continue to come over, so she began massaging Ace's bulge through his pants. He simply smiled and thought how this was normal for Keisha. She then unzipped his pants and felt for his penis. She began to rub it. Kedar kept his eyes on the work, hoping Ace forgot about the money mix-up from the other night. When he was fully aroused, she got down on her hands and knees and put his big dick in her mouth, slurping up and down as if she were starring in the latest installment of *Pimps Up-Hoes Down*. Ace tried to play it cool, but Keisha's head-shot was so intense, that he quickly came all over her face.

She just slurped it all up with no shame, kindly got up and went upstairs to wash. Still enjoying the waves of busting a quick nut, Ace smiled her way and shook his head. He put his dick away, zipped his pants and went back to bagging dope.

Two minutes later, Rick walked in to help with the bagging. He asked Ace if he was okay.

"Man look, later we'll go to the Westside and see what's up with Terrence. If they want beef then beef it is."

Rick loved it. Not only was he Ace's right hand, but he was also another loose cannon.

Ace hollered for Keisha to get downstairs so that she could take Kedar's car and drop off the work. "Tell them niggas Rick will be by to pick up that money on Saturday," he ordered.

## The Lies Hustlers Never Tell

Bitches be swearin' they ballin'
In their wig weaves and knock-off gear
Rollin' in their Caprices
Tinted Hondas or Luminas
Got on dark shades
Poppin' pills
Beefin' with the next chick
'Cause she too is fake
And that's how you feel
Fake ass ballin' bitch
See whores drop their draws for shit they can afford
When these lame hustlin' cats need to be ignored
Puffin' weed, puffin' weed
Bitch breathe, bitch breathe
Sayin' that's your little brother
But that shit's make believe
Late night down low
That's the same nigga you skeeze
Fake ass ballin' bitch

Claim you livin' lavish
Bitch still livin' averge
Scopin' out a nigga for cabbage,
Givin' up straight garbage
Bar hop, club hop
Sayin' the Henney made you do it
Swallowin' straight fluid
Fake bitch
Ballin' trick
All for some other chick's dick
And you still don't get it
Fake ass ballin' bitch
See the fake bitch never changes
Just the slick shit and the penis
Bitches still ballin'
No knowledge, no condom
You bitches better wake up
Gettin' stuck with bastard babies
Low t-cells and fucked up sheets
Ain't a bitch alive that can beat the streets,

*FAKE ASS BALLIN' BITCH*

Nikki had been throwing up for over ten minutes at home in the bathroom. *It's too late to go to Rite Aid for a pregnancy test tonight,* she decided, *but first thing in the morning,* I'm getting one. She called Ace and the phone rang and rang, but he didn't answer. She began to cry and thought about how it was her fault what happened that night and how she shouldn't have gone to the game. Her second thought was the girl and her crew who called Ace's name as he dealt with her. She didn't remember where she knew the loud-mouth girl from.

The ringing of the phone interrupted her thoughts. It was Simone checking to see that Nikki was okay. "Yeah, I'm okay. I'm going to get some rest and I need you to get me a test from Rite Aid in the morning," said Nikki.

"Girl, okay, see you," said Simone.

Nikki tried calling Ace once more before she went to sleep. He picked up. "What's up, babe? Its 2am, why aren't you in bed?"

"I need to talk to you about something, Ace, about something real important. I need to see your face when I tell you," said Nikki.

"What," Ace asked, "You pregnant?"

"No," snapped Nikki. "If I am, I will be getting an abortion."

"Yo, I'ma holla' at you later 'cause you keep talkin' stupid, and I'ma have to do somethin' to you. I'll call you in the mornin'," he said and hung up. Nikki began to cry, and wondered how one once so sweet and warm could be so cold now.

Ace left Rick and Kedar to finish up the business while he headed over to Samira's. Although they weren't together technically, he had a key to where he paid the mortgage. She dared not mess with anyone else. She lived in Newcastle, in the Boothhurst development where there was nothing but single homes. He was driving Rick's Acura, which was in Nadirah's name, and parked it in the driveway. Turning off his phone as he put his key in the door, he removed his shoes once he entered the dark, quiet home.

He went straight to the kitchen to get a bottle of water from the refrigerator and left the grocery money on the kitchen table where Samira was sure to see it. He crept upstairs and went directly to the bathroom to shower. The hot water beating down on his back helped him to relax. Minutes later, he climbed in the bed next to Samira. He moved close to her and remembered the days when they were truly together. Wanting to revisit that place when she slept without underwear, he gently put his fingers between her legs and opened them up. The scent of her made him rise.

Samira stirred awake from his touch and although she wanted to resist, she missed him. As he turned her over on her back, Ace kissed all over her body, from her breasts to her belly button. He slid her legs open a little wider and began to lick and slurp her clitoris. She moaned quietly as he slid his tongue swiftly in and out her vagina. Then he stopped and gently penetrated her. With both of them totally caught up in the moment and holding each other tight, Ace whispered how much he missed her love and begged her to get it back.

"Please, Samira, I need you in my life. Can you give me one more chance? Please, baby?" he pleaded as tears rolled from his eyes.

They kissed passionately, his wet face brushing against hers. After reaching their individual heights together, Ace simply held Samira and told her stories of his past and how he wanted out of the streets now. Samira listened, thinking, *why is this nigga lying*? They drifted off to sleep in each other's arms.

He awoke to sausage, eggs and pancakes the next morning and he couldn't help but think that was what he'd been missing. Samira however, showed no emotion in regards to the night before, and she informed Ace that she would not be going bowling with him and little Ali.

"I forgot I have a sewing class to go to," she lied.

She knew that if in his presence for too long, she would fall victim to his slickness. Ace looked puppy dog sad ,but she just gave him his food and went upstairs to shower and dress. As he ate breakfast, he called his mom to make sure she had gotten his rental. The keys were waiting for him on the mantle.

\*\*\*

Jolting Nikki from what was already an un-restful sleep, the phone rang. It was Simone calling from Rite Aid. "I'ma get this test."

"Okay," said Nikki. "Come through the back door." She quickly got up and opened the door, then went to the bathroom to wash up.

Ace called Rick to see where he was. He wanted to give him back his car so he could get the rental from his mother's house.

"Yo, Richard! Where you at?" asked Ace.

"Home," said Rick. "Stop it with that Richard shit, Ali."

"Alright," said Ace. "I'll be by to get you in ten minutes. One."

"I won't have the mortgage until Friday," Ace said because she didn't want to go bowling.

"Okay," she responded with no anger and totally ignoring his pickiness. She knew him like a book. If he didn't do anything else, he made sure she and their son had a roof over their heads.

Just as father and son walked out of the door Hashim called.

"Yo, Ace, why the hell you turn the game out like that, brother?"

"Man, look, I'm sorry," said Ace. "Did you win or what?

My money was ridin' on you."

"The game was forfeited, because we got to fighting the other team once the crowd started running. It was wild, man," said Hashim. We're supposed to play them next week at the Bob Carpenter Center."

"I'll call you back after me and my son come back from bowlin'.

Sorry, again about the game. Hit me later," he said as he stopped in front of Rick's apartment.

"Yo, Rick, I'm out front," Ace chirped.

"Good lookin' out, Rick," Ace said as Rick approached the car. " You always have my back."

"See you, tonight, One," said Rick dropping Ace and his son in front of Ace's mom's.  He spent the whole day with little Ali, so of course, he turned his phone off.

***

While Samira cleaned the house, trying to take her mind off of things, she debated whether she would check Ace's messages. She decided she needed a sign as to his true intentions. She picked up the phone to call him but ended up punching in his code, just to listen. There were more messages from Nikki and other women.

"It's me, Nikki, I really need to talk to you." Beeeep.

"Yo, yo, it's Tasha, you met me at the gas station last weekend.  Call me, I wanna' see you about somethin', 555-4242." Beeeep.

Disgusted, she called her Muslim sister, Zulema. "As Salaam Alaikum," Zulema greeted.

"Wa Lakum Salaam," replied Samira.. "What are you doing?"

"Nothing," said Zulema.

"Come over so we can study for our Arabic class," Samira suggested.

"Inshallah," said Zulema. "Oh yeah, my mother got you some Godiva chocolates; I'll bring them to you when I come over, Inshallah."

Samira laid on her pillows in the living room as she waited for Zulema. She reminisced on how things were with Ali before the streets took hold of him. Since his father died, her father, being the upstanding and well-respected man he was, took Ali under his wings to teach him how to be a man. He also taught him about the deen of Islam and groomed him to be a righteous Muslim. But, her father became very ill as they came of age, and that's when Ali turned to the streets for his answers. To make matters worse, Samira became pregnant, which angered her father but by then, the streets had Ace by a grip.

She thought about how they enjoyed the family outings together when they were young and how they used to talk about getting married some day. There were so many happy days before the streets. She had loved him since she was twelve years old. And just knew he was going to be her husband.

She remembered that once little Ali was born, they were to get married and he was to work in her family's business. That's also when her parents helped her buy the house in Boothhurst.

The phone ringing released her from her trance. She glanced at the caller ID to see it was AII's mom. "Hi 'Mir, can little Ali stay tonight?" asked Mrs. Prince.

"Yes," answered Samira.

After some small talk, they ended the conversation. Samira heard Ace enter his mom's house as she hung up the phone.

Loud knocking at the door was how Keisha started her day after a long night of doing runs for Ace. "Bitch, get up! You know it's a party at Utopia tonight and we in that motherfucker. You can't wear sneakers, either! Everybody will be there." Jasmine brought not only the plans for the night, but also the ruckus.

"Stop all that noise. I'm still tired from last night," Keisha said, drowsily. "Pass me my phone." Jasmine obliged.

"Yo, Ace, it's me Keisha. What's up for tonight? The boy, Little Trapp is having an album release party for the boy KJ from Newcastle."

"Yeah, well, put on your best; I need you to get with that little pretty nigga from the North-side, Little UC. He ridin' around with Spreewells on a Hummer like shit is so sweet. I need you to do you and find out how much he eatin' and where he stash his work."

"Alright," said Keisha. "I'm on my way to the mall to get somethin'."

"One," said Ace. Since Keisha knew how to play her cards, Ace always sicked her on niggas.

"Yo, Rick, I need to use your car," Keisha chirped on his phone. I got a few jobs to do for Ace tonight," Keisha informed Rick, just before running upstairs to slide into her skin-tight Enyce jeans and a white tee. Moments later, Rick pulled up and gave Keisha the car. He on the other hand, went in her house to sleep, after a long night of doing runs for Ace.

***

Simone brought the pregnancy test to Nikki, as promised. She heard sniffles coming from the bathroom. "Nikki, open up the door," pleaded Simone. "Things will be okay. We can get through this shit together. Just open the door."

Nikki opened the door, still lying on the floor, with an unstoppable stream of tears flowing from her eyes. "What am I going to do, girl?" Nikki sniffled. "I haven't even finished school yet. My dad will have a fit."

"Whatever you decide to do, I'm here for you, okay girl?" Simone comforted. "Look girl, let's go to the mall. Maybe you'll feel a little better if we spend some money. But we need to go through the West-side first so I can see if my peoples is gonna give me a couple a dollars."

Simone sounded sweet, but her motives were anything but sweet. Terrence said he would pay Simone if she could hook him up with Nikki.

"Let's ride in my car," said Nikki. "While I get dressed, go to your house and get some money. By the time you get back, I'll be ready."

"Alright," agreed Simone. "Don't take all day. I'll only be ten minutes."

Nikki got up from the floor and washed her face before calling Ace from the edge of her bed. "Ace, it's me, Nikki. I really need to talk to you about some important stuff. Can you please call me? I love you." She slid on just some sweat pants and a plain tee-shirt. Simone was pulling up just as Nikki walked out the door.

"You drive," she said.

"I don't feel like it."

As they drove down Market Street, Alicia Keys promised to keep her lover's secrets. They turned off Fourth Street onto Madison and ran smack dead into Terrence.

"Brother, what's up?" greeted Simone. Terrence's face still swollen from the blows of the night before, looked to see who was in the truck.

"Girl, don't be pullin' up on me like that," he warned. "You about to go to the mall?" He reached in his pocket and pulled out a wad of money. "How much you need?"

"Only like, two hundred," Simone replied.

"Oh, I'm sorry; what's up Nikki?" Terrence asked, pretending to just notice her, "You goin' to the mall, too?"

"Yes," Nikki simply replied.

"Well, here's two hundred for you, too," he smiled as he passed her two crisp one hundred dollar bills. "You can have whatever you want," he went on. "You know I been likin' you. When you gonna let me take you to dinner or at least get your number?"

Nikki smiled and said, "You know I'm with Ace, so I can't do that. Plus you saw what happened to me at the game last night."

"Yeah, look at me," Terrence said, holding the side of his lumped up face. "He got that for now. I'm just waitin' for the right moment. When you ready to be treated right, call me."

As they rolled off the set, Kedar was turning the corner, just in time to see Nikki's Lexus pull away from Terrence. With the quickness, he called Ace.

"Yo, your girl with the Lex' just rode through Fifth Street talkin' to that boy," Kedar reported.

"What, what you say?" asked Ace.

"Man, your girl with the Lex', the college jawn, was just on Fifth Street smilin' all in Terrence's face," Kedar reported still trying to get on Ace's good side from the whole money situation.

"Good, lookin'," said Ace, his face red. "I'ma fuck this bitch up if she keep on playin'," he fumed. That's why I do what I do, cause a bitch gonna' be a bitch.

Nikki and Simone parked by the food court entrance at the mall. They noticed a group of girls staring, but paid them no particular attention. They got out the car and walked towards the mall. Keisha remembered the Lexus and the tags from the night of the game, so she followed. Nikki, busy eyeing the outfit in the window of Banana Republic, didn't even notice Keisha when she called out Ace's name just to be funny. Simone heard her.

Simone turned to see a little skinny girl with a long weave

and tight jeans, but she just rolled her eyes and followed Nikki into the store. Seeing that she did not get to either Nikki or Simone, Keisha decided on another tactic. She bumped right into Nikki, as if by accident. Nikki, still oblivious to what was going on, continued to shop.

"Look, girl, these pants are on sale finally," Simone pointed out to Nikki, paying Keisha no attention. Trying to think of something even more devious, Keisha rolled her eyes and walked out the store. She reconnected with her girls and left the mall.

With the whole crew in the parking lot, Jasmine snapped. "Key Ace's car since that bitch wanna' ride!"

"Yeah, sounds good to me," Keisha said pumped up. She took the key to Rick's car and scraped it across the Lexus, criss-crossing the paint from front to back, top to bottom. She and Jasmine even played a game of tic-tac-toe across the hood.

When Simone and Nikki left the mall, Simone was the first to notice. "I know that ain't your car lookin' like that!" she said in disbelief.

"Oh, shit!" screamed Nikki, "What the hell happened to my car?"

Twenty minutes later, Ace called. "Yo Nikki, babe, where you at?"

"I'm at the mall," she informed him. "Someone just keyed my car so I'm actually waiting for the police to file a report for my insurance company."

"Oh-call me back once things get straightened out with the car," Ace said, seeming totally unconcerned.

Simone and Nikki were pissed as they sat and waited for the police. All they could do was sit on the curb and stare at the car.

"Look girl, did you peep that girl followin' us in the store?" Simone asked Nikki.

"No, what girl?" asked Nikki.

"The brown-skinned chick with the long weave," Simone went on.

"Girl, you trippin'," Nikki said.

Simone switched directions. "Look Nikki, we need to find out some scoop on Ace, especially since you're pregnant. You don't even know his real name, not to mention, his address. I went to school with Nadirah and her brother, Hashim, who is real cool with Ace. I'll get her number some time this weekend."

"Alright," said Nikki, still clueless and feeling out of sorts because she missed Ace.

***

Rick and Ace sat in the dining room at Keisha's house, planning things for the night and waiting for her to come home.

"Man, niggas need to come up with that change or shit needs to get ugly," said Rick . We also need to handle that West-side shit before it gets out of hand. You know that boy, Terrence play real dirty," he warned. "He gets his car detailed every Sunday, while he's at the baseball game, so I got that end.

"As far the dough goes, let's give niggas a few more days and then we put the pressure on 'em," said Ace.

Keisha walked in all smiles, expecting to see only Rick. "Sweetie, here's your car" she said stopping dead in her tracks when she saw Ace. It was as if she had seen a ghost.

"Yo, what the fuck is wrong with you keyin' up that Lexus like that?" Ace demanded as he grabbed her by her weave and dragged her across the dirty, hardwood floors.

"Stop Ace!" she hollered. "Rick, get your boy!"

Rick simply watched as Ace dragged her all the way to the bedroom. He threw her on the bed and started landing body blows.

"Stop playin'!" he yelled. "Why the hell would you key

my fuckin' car? You stupid bitch. Keep actin' dumb and I'ma cut your dumb ass off! And get ready, I'll be back to get you tonight to go to the party!"

Keisha cried but it was normal for him to hit on her. She almost acted as if she liked it. Nonetheless, she threw a shoe at him in retaliation as he left the room.

"Stupid bitch!" he spat as he slammed the bedroom door.

On his way out the door, Ace called Nikki.

"Yes, Ace," she answered somewhat sarcastically, but cautiously. She was still a bit irritated by his indifference towards her car.

"Yo, where you at?" he questioned.

"Home," Nikki responded. Satisfied she was where he wanted her.

"I need to use the Lexus tonight."

"Didn't I tell you it was scratched up. Probably by one of your bitches."

"So you scratched up the car yourself," Ace joked, " 'Cause you're the only person I'm with at the moment. That nigga Terrence probably did the shit since he's a bitch but I'ma handle that this week, for sure. See the bullshit you caused all because you wanted to go to the game?" he accused; although his beef with Terrence had been going on since grade school.

Definitely back in check, Nikki said, "I really need to talk to you, Ace. You need to allot some time for me, just you and me."

"I'm busy handlin' business at the moment, babe, but I'll get with you later and then we can talk."

"Alright," Nikki said disappointed. "I'm about to get some rest anyway, so I'll call you once I wake up. I love you."

He had promised to tuck in little Ali after his bath, so Ace headed home to his mom's.

"Mom, did Samira call?" he asked as soon as stepped in the door.

"Naa, sweetie; I haven't spoken to her since earlier, just before you dropped Ali off," responded Mrs. Prince with care.

After tucking in Ali, Ace felt stressed and needed to clear his head. He took a ride on the highway with Alicia Keys blasting "*...some people want diamond rings/ some just want everything/but everything means nothing/if I ain't got you...*" He thought of Samira and their conversation from the morning. He knew the right thing to do was to honor her. He also felt he still had time to burn.

"Yo Ace, Kedar just got shot over the Westside! Meet me at Crozier Hospital in Chester!" Rick's voice blasted through the phone.

"One," said Ace as he turned the car around to head north towards PA. Kedar is always doin' some dumb shit. Now I'ma really have to bang this nigga Terrence out," Ace concluded.

Keisha called Ace but the voice-mail picked up on the first ring, "Yo it's me. I'm about to leave for the party; it's almost eleven and the party ends at two. So I'm leavin' without you."

Jasmine and Keisha entered Utopia sharp as ever. Keisha was a project chick with a cute face, slim build and fat ass. She wore a backless dress so that her tattoo was visible; the four Aces from a deck of cards with the words 'Aces are wild' emblazoned across her back. As soon as they came in, she spotted UC from the North-side; *bling-blingin' as usual, with his sharp self,* she thought.

She walked right up to him at the bar where he was talking to another girl, "Drinks on you, UC?" she cut in without excusing herself.

UC, always smiling, said, "Of course, is that all you want?"

"Naa," Keisha leaned in close and whispered in his ear. "It's a lot of fries that come with this shake I got." She walked away carrying the apple martini he had gotten her, swinging her ass hard enough to spill a little of the drink. She knew he was watching, though. She also knew that if that didn't work, then her come-fuck-me dress never failed. She mingled with a few people as she walked towards the dance floor, gulping down the drink along the way. She danced erotically; feeling on herself and staring at UC. Not really thinking with the head on his shoulders, he went towards the dance floor to join her.

On his way, he leaned towards his cousin Amir and said, "Yo, I'm fuckin' that tonight, for sure." As they danced, Keisha stayed close to him, making sure her ass kept contact with his rock solid crotch. "You with me tonight?" asked UC, smiling devilishly. "You know it," she said, hugging him close and sticking her tongue in his ear. While the local rap artist moved the crowd, Keisha acted as if she was drunk, and UC couldn't believe his good luck.

***

When Ace arrived in the waiting room at Crozier, Kedar's mom, Rick, Nadirah, and Black were already there holding vigil. They had already gotten word from the surgeon that Kedar was extremely fortunate and that he would be okay. They all wanted to stick around for a while, just until Kedar's mom decided she was ready to go. Rick pulled Ace aside from the door. He informed Ace that according to Black, he and Kedar were over on the Westside shooting dice when Terrence pulled up talkin' shit. Next thing they knew, shots were ringing through the air. Nobody actually saw who was doing the shooting.

As Ace listened, his face went three shades of red. Then, out of respect, he spent a few moments comforting Mrs. Wilmore before leaving. He made sure to tell Black, with only his eyes, that he was not pleased. He told Rick to call him later, then he was out.

Ace left the hospital to go drop off the money that Rick

had slid him while they were visiting. He hardly ever went to his Aunt Karin's house out in Delaware City just to visit; that's where he kept his money. He only went there about once every two weeks. Sometimes he sent Samira, either to drop money off or to pick it up.

As soon as he stepped through the door, he went straight to his stash and began to count it. *Damn, this shit is low,* he thought. Happy his aunt was still at the hair salon she owned, he finished what he was doing and fell asleep on the couch. The streets were really beginning to bug him, but the rush was impossible to leave.

***

After a passion-filled night of opening up, or rather laying it down on UC, Keisha awakened in the Presidential suite at the Wyndham Hotel. He was already awake and smiling. "What's up for the day? Wanna' go shoppin' or what?" he inquired.

Keisha smiled, knowing she must have done her job last night and said, "Of course."

"Ace, won't be mad, will he?" he questioned.

"Hell, no," said Keisha. "I'm not with him anymore, he's just my baby daddy."

Their conversation was interrupted by UC's phone. "Little UC, where you at, man?" Amir checked for his cousin through the Nextel.

"I'm still with the babe, Keisha. I'll hit you later," said UC.  "Man, fuck that ho', its money to be made. Anyway, ain't she with that nigga Ace from the Villa?" Amir questioned angrily.  "Naa, man, she with me; you know how we do cousin," said Little UC jokingly.

"One," said Amir.

He turned to Keisha without saying a word, picked her up and carried her into the bathroom. The marble sunken tub was

41

filled to nearly overflowing with bubbles, and candles were lit everywhere casting a romantic glow on the walls. They relaxed in the tub for a couple luxurious hours with UC bathing Keisha from head-to-toe, making sure he stopped often to lick and kiss whatever body part he was cleansing at the time. When they got out of the tub and as UC wrapped Keisha in the fluffiest, softest, towel she had ever felt. he led her to the dining area where he had arranged to have a hot breakfast waiting for them. Keisha, who normally had a whole lot to say, was utterly speechless.

They hit the highway heading towards Philadelphia, South Street. "What store do you want to hit first?" UC questioned.

"Barefeet," said Keisha. "To get a pair of shoes." She was real psyched because Ace never took her anywhere just to spend some cash; UC however, felt, bullshit bitches like bullshit things.

"Yo Keisha, none of the shoes in that store are leather; let me turn you on to a spot. Let's leave South Street."

They ended up at a little boutique on Main Street in Manayunk. Keisha's eyes were huge as she took everything in. Nothing in the store was less than two hundred-fifty dollars.

"Get what you want," said UC. "I like my woman stylish," he said. Keisha was as excited as a kid in a candy store with all the good shit up front, and she couldn't figure out why he was treating her so nice. *Damn, this is what dealin' with a real baller is like*, she thought, as she put two pair of Prada boots and a pair of Gucci loafer's on the counter. She tried the shoes on so fast that the saleswoman got excited knowing this was going to be an easy, painless sale.

UC got himself two pair of Bruno MaglI's just for kicks.

"Will this be cash or credit?" asked the saleslady, eyes wide as she calculated her commission on the quick $3400 sale.

Keisha's jaw hit the floor when UC counted out $4000 cash, as if it was nothing. And when he told the lady to keep the change, she nearly fainted.

Dollar signs were all Keisha saw and Ace needed to come up. Quickly catching herself, she back-tracked. I do love him at times, she reflected, even though he treats me like shit. Nobody even knew that she fronted him money from time-to-time and she would never tell; especially since everyone in the city thought he was baller of all ballers…

"Did you hear me?" asked UC, waking her from her day-dream. "I said," he repeated, "Don't you need some outfits to funk with them shoes?"

"Yo," called Amir on the phone. "Where you at? We here at the studio waitin' on you and shit? What the fuck you doin'? I know you ain't still with that bitch?"

"Stop disrespectin' my peoples like that. I'll be there soon. I'm already in Philly anyway," UC said frustrated with Amir and his attitude towards Keisha.

Turning back to her as he navigated the traffic through the streets of Philadelphia, en route to Roosevelt Boulevard, he said, "Listen babe, I'm not going to be able to take you to get the out-fits, but I want you to get some nice shit to wear with those shoes for me. So here, will this be enough to get something nice?" he asked as he peeled off another $1500. "I'm going to go holla at these niggas right quick and I'll get up with you later. I don't know how long I'll be so you take my car," he continued.

Overwhelmed, all Keisha could say was, "Whatever you say, Boo." She didn't want to say too much because she didn't want to sound like she wasn't used to this type of treatment.

"Okay then, give me a kiss," as he reached over and jammed his tongue down her throat. "Damn, you taste good," he said as he got out the car in front of the studio.

Keisha was so pumped up she couldn't wait to get home. She jumped on the highway with a little over 2G's to give to Ace; the $1500 plus her welfare check. She couldn't get to Delaware fast enough.

She burst through the door and ran upstairs once home to put her money under the bed; Rick was in the kitchen cooking cheese-eggs and toast. "Damn, you must have had a long weekend," observed Rick.

"Yeah, you know how I do," said Keisha smiling, as she toted all her bags from her shopping spree to the kitchen. "I'm on my way to the hairdresser before I go out again with that boy."

"So what's the verdict; where that nigga live?" Rick interrogated.

"I got it under control," she assured. "We gonna be rollin' in crazy dough," laughed Keisha.

"Hey babe, it's me Keisha. I put some money under the mattress; you won't believe how I got this boy open."

Ace chirped back, "That's what's up, Bonnie and Clyde for life."

***

Nikki's cell phone jingled just as she was on her way into class, "Hey, babe, you in class yet?"

"Yes," she said excitedly, happy to finally here from Ace.

"I'll be there to get you for lunch," he promised.

"Alright," she said floating to her seat.

***

Simone called Terrence on her way to work to get Hashim's number. "Yo brother," she said coolly. "Since the game got forfeited, I need Hashim's number to find out when the next game is."

Smelling more than what she was saying, Terrence said, "Yeah alright, you always up to somethin', but here's his number."

She thanked Terrence and called Hashim, "Yo, can I get

44

Nadirah's number, Haji?" she asked without identifying herself.

"Who is this and how the hell did you get my number?"

"My bad Haji, it's Simone."

"I'll tell my sister to call you; I'm not giving out her number," he said, protective of his sister.

"Alright, that's fine. I appreciate it," said Simone. True to his word, less than two minutes later, Nadirah returned Simone's call. "I haven't spoken to you in ages; what do you want?" Nadirah asked suspiciously.

"Well, you know the boy Ace is datin' my girl Nikki and I just wanted the scoop on him; plus she might be pregnant by him. But, he hasn't told her nothin' about himself; she doesn't even know his real name," Simone reported.

"Damn, that's a shame," said Nadirah, "so why yyou calling me? The only thing I can tell you is that he's a dog and that he only truly loves one woman, Samira. They have a son together. If your friend is pregnant by him then I feel sorry for her. He considers his son with Samira his only child, so your girl better run while she still can because Ace will snap if Samira finds out," she warned. "He's crazy, so that's my advice to you and your friend. I've got to go."

"Thanks, Nadirah," said Simone appreciatively.

Simone immediately called Nikki to tell her what she had found out about Ace. Nikki saw that it was Simone calling, and sent her straight to voice-mail instead of answering. She was on her way through the library to meet Ace for lunch, so she didn't have time to talk. As she walked out, he was there standing outside his burgundy Dodge Stratus rental. Avant blasted, hoping, wishing and praying for his lady not to take her love away. She smiled as he opened the car door for her and greeted her with a wet kiss. "Damn, I really did miss you," he said, deep-down a little surprised.

They went to TGI Friday's near the campus where Nikki

had ordered two appetizer's, an entree and dessert. "Hungry?" asked Ace, checking the size of the meal she had just begun devouring.

"Yeah," said Nikki, wiping the Jack Daniels sauce from her mouth. "Can I ask you something?"

"Yes," said Ace.

"Do you ever think about having a family, a wife and kids?" smiled Nikki.

"Of course," Ace responded offensively. "But right now, things ain't right. When I get straight, I'll have my family."

*I already have a family in Samira and Ali,* he confirmed to himself.

"Why did you ask me that anyway?"

"Just wondering," smiled Nikki as she took a big bite of her juicy steak. *It's going to be sooner than he thinks,* she thought.

Ace watched as Nikki finished sucking down all that food. He reached in his pocket to pay the check and called Rick at the same time, ~*chirp*~ "Meet me at Simone's. Did you pick up the loot?" he asked.

"Yeah, I'm on the block now gettin' our money from these niggas, so by the time you get here I'll be ready. One," said Rick.

"Ace, why don't you ever respond to any of my messages?" asked Nikki.

"Man, I don't even check them messages. I think it's somethin' wrong with my voice-mail," he gamed her up. "So, if you don't catch me directly, don't leave a message."

"Why?"

"What did you say?"

"Nothing important," she said, afraid to tell him she was pregnant after his cold response to her question about family. He dropped her off back at school, with a short, "Call me later, babe." Then he pulled off, bumpin' corners as if he were in a rush.

46

Simone sat on her steps smoking a cigarette, contemplating if she should tell Nikki what she'd heard. She didn't want her friend to get played, but maybe she shouldn't say anything. Her thoughts were interrupted by Rick coming up the block, "What up, Simone? Give me a pull of that Newport."

"Damn nigga, with as much money as you gettin', you need to be buyin' me a carton of Newports," she complained as she passed him the cigarette. "You better not get too close anyway; Nadirah might ride by," she went on, with a smirk on her face and staring Rick up and down.

"Go 'head with that shit," he said. "Nadirah don't rule me. Anyway, Ace is supposed to be meetin' me here in a little bit."

"What's up with your boy Ace? He tryin' to play my girl?" she asked.

"Man, we sure ain't gonna' discuss my man or his business. If your girl don't know what time it is, she better borrow your watch," he laughed way harder than necessary, holding his stomach.

"Oh you got jokes, huh, nigga?" Simone smacked her lips pissed, because she did not find him that funny.

Meanwhile, Ace pulled up, "Hop in Rick. What up Simone? I see you lookin' sexy like always; lips all glossed up. *Uuuuuuuhh, I like it like that,*" he serenaded as they drove off, agreeing with Juvenile who was blasting from the radio.

They cruised down Fourth towards the West-side, when they spotted Terrence on his way into the Chinese restaurant at Fourth and Madison. Ace had already pulled over before Terrence even noticed; by then it was too late.

"Yo T, let me holla at you for a second." Agitated, Terrence turned around quickly and started spilling, "Man look, I don't want beef and I didn't shoot your man, either." "Man look, we both got a lot to lose if we go to war and a lotta people would get hurt, for sure. So I don't know about you, but I'm tryin' to get money.

"Let's squash this petty beef so we can go back to our loot," Ace suggested.

"Man look, I didn't mean any disrespect, word? I didn't know the babe was your girl. And Kedar knows it wasn't me who shot him; it was that punk-ass Mike, over a football game from last winter," Terrence confessed.

Down for whatever, Rick was on stand-by, outside the car with his hand on his Glock, just in case. Ace gestured for him to chill because the beef was squashed. "Alright T, that's what's up. And about the bitch, ain't no hard feelin's; we both players and from time-to-time we may bump heads."

Terrence looked puzzled because Ace wasn't the type to make peace first. "Alright," agreed Terrence still pretty hesitant.

"Yeah," Ace went on, "so our crews know it's over, we can get Little Trapp to give a West-side/East-side party at The Lounge." They shook hands to seal the truce.

\*\*\*

Nikki returned Simone's call as she was leaving school and getting into her car, "Hey girl, what's up?"

"Nothin'," said Simone.

"I talked to Nadirah and she said Ace has a girlfriend and a child."

"What? I know about the son but how can he have a girl-friend when he's always with me?"

"Look, I don't know but Nadirah ain't gonna lie. You need to check that nigga," said Simone emphatically.

"Girl, let me hit you back once I get in the house," said Nikki. On the drive home, she called Ace; and of course, *no answer.*

## CHAPTER 4

## A Bitch is a Bitch

They call me fake ass ballin' bitch
Hangin' with major figure niggas
Some even call me a thoroughbred
'Cause of the way I carry bricks
Coochies stuffin' down for the get down
Be it in a ride or Greyhound
Pound for motherfuckin' pound
Side by side
Some may hate 'cause of the way I carry the weight
Using my ass as bait
Thinkin' you gettin' pussy, but you just got raped
'Cause I'm that motherfuckin' bitch
From day one when you broke
Let's get it nigga'
'Till you motherfuckin' rich
Lace me; Fendi, Gabbana
African, have them thinkin' I'm Italian
Ride or die nigga
I'm with you
True bitch 'till the end
I cock back and blast first
Baddest bitch in a skirt
For my nigga, I put in work
Who got your back?
Relax
What? Who want it?
Fat ass, big tits
Shiiiiiitttt!
Set up any for the penny
Without a gun
I'm his side chick
Ride or die click, hit or miss
His number one bitch
A bitch is a bitch,
And I'm it!

## A BITCH IS A BITCH

Ace answered the phone on the fourth ring. "Yo, babe, it's me Keisha. I'm in the boy UC's house and it is definitely like that! It's like some *MTV Cribs*-type shit," Keisha reported excitedly.

"Oh? Where that pretty nigga at?" Ace asked perking up. "And thanks for that dough."

"He left me here while he went to get breakfast for us," said Keisha, lying naked in his California king-size bed surrounded by blue furry pillows with exquisite blue linens. *This is the life*, thought Keisha, *a big change from my full-size mattress on the floor.*

"So why not hit his ass now?" Ace asked, feeling a bit warm and anxious.

"Nigga calm down. You want a little bit of shit or do you wanna' get it all?" asked Keisha. "Just be patient. I got you, and I always will. What's the problem? Or are you really actin' like that because you miss me or somethin'?" laughed Keisha.

"Look, stop playin' games, man. I need to come up. Shit is tight right now and the bills keep comin'. Call me back when you got some good news." Ace hung up in her ear..

"Who was that you were talking to, Keish?" UC asked as he walked into the bedroom, startling her.

"Uh, my oldest son, Richard, callin' from his grandmother's house," she recouped.

"Here's some salmon and eggs from Haneefa's Kitchen and some Akbar tea. I hope you made yourself at home." "Of course. So, what are we doin' today?" Keisha asked as she ran her fingers through his curly hair.

Getting aroused, he said, "Well today is a chill day for me. We can just cool out, and go catch a movie or something. When you get through eating, put this Baby Phat sweat-suit on with these S Dots," UC said handing her yet another shopping bag.

"Damn, so I don't even have to go home to change. That's what's up, babe!" Keisha said surprised and truly thankful. She was leaning over to give him a kiss when the doorbell rang. UC reluctantly pulled away and went downstairs to answer the door. Amir stepped in with, "Yo, you ready? We got to go back to the studio before we go to Vegas." UC looked as if he didn't know what the hell was going on.

"Oh yeah," he said, "I almost forgot. I got company, give me a second."

He went back upstairs, "Hey babe, you got a babysitter for the rest of the week so that you can go to Vegas with me and my peoples?" With no hesitation, she jumped at the chance, "Hell yeah!" Keisha exclaimed. She had only been to Vegas on drug runs, but now she could go for fun.

"I want to take you on a gondola ride through the canals around the Venetian Hotel; it's just like Little Italy. But for now, I have a little more business to take care of around the city. Little Trapp and I have a record label and we have to get the boy from Newcastle, KJ in the studio tonight."

"For real!" Keisha squealed amazed. "I heard some of his shit the other night at the party. He sounds like Jigga. So, you're the owner of UC Trapp Records? They're always on the radio pumpin' your label. I didn't even know that was you!"

"So take the Hummer and make sure you handle your children. Here's some money to get a few things to take with you and if you need to pay a babysitter, let me know," said UC. No one had ever cared whether she had a babysitter or given her money to get prepared for a trip. Her eyes were as big as saucers. She knew she had scored. She grabbed his keys out of his hand and ran out of the door.

Keisha rode through every set in the city, so that every-body could see her in his car. "*....I can make you celebrity overnight...,*" Twista promised her. She stopped to pick up her girls, Jasmine, Nijah and Odaysha. They were already outside her house because it was the hot spot. "Shit must be sweet. What is

Ace gonna' say?" asked Jasmine, knowing Keisha was on a mission for Ace.

"Bitch fuck you. At this moment, Little UC is where it's at," Keisha said as she pulled on the hydro blunt passed through the window.

"Get in y'all, we gonna cruise the sets." None of them had to be asked twice. They all dove into the plush Hummer as if they were going for the gold in the Olympics.

"Bitch, this shit is nice; change the CD," said Nijah steadily pushing every button she could get her hands on.

"Keisha, baby, it's me UC called. See if a few of your friends want to go with us. Make sure they're cute 'cause I'll let them meet Amir, Khaliq, and Dominique." "Alright, babe, I got it covered. My squad is definitely workin'." Keisha passed on the invitation, "Girls, this nigga is major; we goin' to Vegas tonight!" Eminem provided the soundtrack as they cruised "...*these chicks don't even know the name of my band/but they're all on me like they wanna' hold hands/but once I blow they know that I'll be the man....*"

***

Ace and Rick split their earnings.

"Yo, take the rental back to my mom's and drop me off at Samira's. I want to put in some time with her and Ali before we go to Miami," said Ace still counting.

They continued to cruise the East-side, headed toward Southbridge. Riding pass the projects, they saw Keisha in Little UC's Hummer pulling away from the dusty sidewalk, music blasting.

"Damn, you got her trained well!" exclaimed Rick. "The nigga got her in his whip and everything. Did you see the shit he copped her from Philly?"

Unconcerned, Ace replied, "She's my ride or die. However she plays it, she plays it well. So that alone will give us a big ass come up once we hit that nigga." He could taste quick cash, it was so close, that infamous grin appeared on his lips.

Ace jumped out the car to enter Samira's house when Rick realized he had forgotten to go to the spot to pick up some money.

Ace opened the door with his key and greeted Samira as he removed his shoes.

"Ali is still at your mom's, so what's up?" Samira asked.

"I just wanted to spend some time with you alone, is that okay, babe?"

She smiled and threw a pillow at him as she walked back to the kitchen. "I baked some fish; if you'd like some it's in the oven," Samira offered.

"Naa, I'm not hungry. You know I'm goin' to Miami in a few days so I wanted to be with you before I went," said Ace sweetly.

"Well, I'm reading the Quran, so if you're here with me that's what we will be doing," she said firmly, walking into the family room.

"Alright, but let me take a quick shower, first," Ace surrendered then he headed upstairs. Samira felt he loved her and she loved him, but his cheating left her tormented.

While he was in the shower, she checked his messages from her phone. There were a few messages from Keisha, telling him she was going away and that girl, Nikki was still calling and sounding sad. *Too bad he'll never hear these*, she thought, as she erased them all one-by-one.

"Babe, I'm almost done," Ace called from upstairs as he came out the shower. "Look in my pocket and get that money, take half for your account and take the rest to Aunt Karin's."

"Ace, you risk your life and soul for this little bit of change? You're crazy."

"I'm gonna stop soon; word I am. Then we're gonna get married,watch," he promised her as he joined her on the pillows piled up on the floor.

"I'll be married to someone else by the time you decide to change your life," she warned.

Ace's face turned red, "You always spoiling a good moment, with your smart self."

"You're getting mad, but I'm dead serious," said Samira, as she opened the Quran and began reading the parts she hoped would help him find his way back. They studied the Holy Book for a few hours before falling asleep.

***

Keisha was back at home furiously throwing underwear and some clothes into a dusty knapsack when Rick came upstairs.

"Why you so happy Keish?"

"Ahhh, wouldn't you like to know, nigga? Tell Ace I'ma call from the boy's house. He has two alarms. I just haven't gotten the codes yet. But shit is lookin' real sweet for us. This nigga is ballin' like on some big boy shit," she said excitedly but played it cool.

Then remembering what UC instructed her to do, "Damn Rick, do me a favor. I'ma get some things ready for the kids. Can you take it pass my mother's and tell Ace that Richard needs a coat?" Rick was ordinarily much more accommodating than Ace when it came to children. He loved the kids and would do anything for them, even if they weren't his, while Ace, on the other hand only showed emotion for little Ali.

"You tell Ace what the kids need; if he wants me to get it, then I will, but I ain't gettin' into that shit with you and him anymore," he complained. Then his heart for the children kicked in. "I am goin' that way, so I'll take the stuff, but I ain't no motherfuckin' runner!" he barked.

Fed up, Keisha got right with him. "Stop bitchin' like a girl! I'm puttin' in major work for you niggas. Not to mention this cat is from our own city, it ain't like before with a outta' town cat, so just do it damn!"

That's exactly why Keisha didn't want Ace or Rick to know she would be having fun, being wined and dined. "Ace wants you to call before you leave," said Rick.

Hoooonk! Jasmine blew from the street. "Come on, girl, so we can all get ready!" she hollered from the window of the Hummer.

Rick walked to the door while Keisha was still upstairs, having forgotten a few more things. His eyes got big, "Damn, Keish, you good. That nigga trust your silly ass with his Hummer? What you doin' a run or somethin'," said Rick still pushing it.

"Fuck you Rick, I'm good for somethin' more than just business," said Keisha offended. She drew the conclusion that, these niggas really didn't appreciate her or the risks she took for them. She hurried out the door and told Rick to call Ace because she didn't have time. She hopped in the car and joined Beyonce in calling all the names of her naughty girls. They peeled off the dusty project road onto the street.

Nijah and Odaysha were dropped off first, so they could go get ready. "I'll be back-I'm goin' to the mall. UC gave up some cash so I could get a few things. Call me once you girls are ready," she said.

"Alright," they sang in unison as they got out of the car. Jasmine, on the other hand, said she needed to go to the mall too. She really wanted to know her girl's motives with Little UC because she was looking a little too happy.

"Keish, so what's the deal?" she asked.

"What girl? We're just goin' to have fun," said Keish giving away nothing.

"Girl, I know that look in your eyes," she pressed, "that's the same look you had when you met Ace. I wish you would stop lettin' these niggas game you up. Take them for what they're worth," Jasmine said seriously.

"I got this," said Keisha, never heeding anyone's advice.

Nikki called Ace from work, but as usual she got his voice mail. "Babe, it's me. I know you said you don't check your messages but just in case, please call me. We need to talk," she whined. Nikki wanted to talk to Ace very badly, so she could ask him about what Simone had told her earlier. Deep inside she knew her friend wouldn't tell her anything untrue, but she also wanted to believe this man she had fallen so hard for.

A phone call from her mom interrupted her thoughts, "Yes Mom, I'm at work," she answered dryly.

"Your father picked your car up from the garage but the insurance company said they wouldn't pay for it, since you couldn't prove it was vandalized," Nikki's mom updated her. "And what's wrong, sweetie? You don't sound too good."

"Nothing, Mom, I'll be home soon. Love you." Nikki's eyes began to water because she wanted to tell her mother that she was pregnant, but she didn't want to disappoint her parents, either. They had saved for her education all her life and a baby would keep her from accomplishing her goals. *And how much more proof does the insurance company need than tic-tac-toe all over my damn hood!* Nikki thought really getting what her mom said about her car.

On the way home from work, Nikki decided to stop by Simone's. She sat on the front steps, in the usual spot.

"Girl, you seen Ace?" asked Nikki.

"Naa," said Simone. "Not since earlier when he came to get Rick.

Did you get to ask him about his baby moms?" "Naa, I

keep trying to call him but his phone is off, as always," Nikki replied exasperated.

"I want to at least catch him before they go on their trip."

"Girl, you better get an abortion and keep it movin'. Ace is not the nigga to have a baby by. You can't even catch his ass now. Plus, you're in school tryin' to get your degree. That baby shit is extra and a part-time job won't cut it," Simone advised.

"I heard that," is all Nikki said to keep from exploding. She was angry that Simone kept drilling her with the fact that Ace was no good. "Well, girl, I've got to go home to study for an exam. I'll catch you later," she said as she turned to get back into her car.

*They would be playing this sad ass song on the radio right now,* Nikki thought without attempting to change the station Amanda Perez was singing her heart out. "...*God sent me and Angel/from the Heavens above/sent me an angel/ to heal my broken heart/from being in love/'cause all I do is cry/God sent me an angel to wipe the tears from my eyes...*" Nikki began to cry uncontrollably. By the time she got home, her eyes were so puffy it looked as if she had gone a couple rounds in the ring.

Keisha and her crew arrived at UC's all stirred up and excited to get out of the city. ~*chirp*~ "Babe, we're outside and ready to roll," Keisha said, barely containing herself.

"Alright sexy," replied UC, "Leave your girls outside in the car and you come in for a second. I got some shit I wanna show you." Keisha hopped out the Hummer with the quickness just as Amir was walking up.

"Ill, nasty," he said, half teasing but mostly serious.

Keisha looked at him and sucked her teeth. "You just mad 'cause I ain't fuck you back in the day, nigga; get over it and stop actin' like a bitch." She shut him up for the moment. UC met her at the door with open arms and she embraced him smiling and flicking her tongue in and out of his ear while cutting her eyes towards Amir. "What you got for me babe?"

He said nothing, but she followed his gaze. A stretch Hummer pulled up and parked behind UC's.

"Damn!" Keisha exclaimed, no longer holding in her excitement. "We doin' it like that?"

"You better believe it," said UC as he led her into the house. "Listen to me Keisha," he said staring her in her eyes, attempting to touch her heart. "I've liked you since the ninth grade but you started fuckin' with that Ace character, so I fell back. Not to mention, you got pregnant and didn't come back to school, so I waited patiently. Now I got you. I know you're not used to being treated as well as I treat you, nor will you ever be. I just wanted you to know that."

Keisha was genuinely touched but all she knew to do- was her. "Well I'm feelin' you too," she said placing his hand on her ass. "This is all you, daddy, all you. Don't worry."

Not being able to stand all the love and just hatin' in general, Amir stuck his head in the door, "Man, come on; you two can get it on once we hit Nevada. Let's go!"

Keisha played UC really close as he entered the code for the alarm. "You can wait in the car babe, I'll be there in a minute," he said over his shoulder.

"I don't wanna' be without you for even one minute," she purred seductively, keeping her eyes on what he was doing. *Got it ! One down and three to go,* she thought to herself.

UC locked up and they headed towards the limo, just in time to catch Dominique's Nas imitation "...*Oochie wally wally/oochie bang bang...*" as he watched Jasmine's ass swing in her terry cloth Baby Phat sweat suit.

# CHAPTER 5

## Caught Up

Samira and Ali gave their baby a standing ovation for his part in his first school play. "I enjoy doin' family things with you, babe," Ace whispered. "We should do these things more often,he said "as he put his arm around Samira.

Removing his arm, she flatly replied, "Would you please take us straight home after this is over, Ace?" Deep inside, Samira wanted to be with him, but her faith in Allah gave her the strength to reject him. She was getting a little tired of making sacrifices for him. It truly was a struggle enjoying the good and forbidding the evil when it came to the love of her life.

"We had a good few days and now you're changin' as if you did-n't know I was goin' away. You made the reservations so what's wrong?

What did I do now?" Ace asked clearly frustrated.

"I'm not trippin' off you going away. You've taken me away many times so that's not my gripe," said Samira, feeling her own frustration. "I just want you to change for little Ali, if not for yourself. When are you going to change? When will enough be enough?" Samira questioned without really expecting an answer.

On the way home they listened too Ruben 'Big Rube' Studdard apologize a million times because he was so sorry. When Ace pulled into Samira's driveway, he barely got a chance to fully stop the car before she swung open the door and practi-cally jumped out. Before slamming it shut she asked, "How many times can you be sorry?"

Ace blushed shamefully as he trailed her in the house.

"Yo 'Mir, I *do* love you; any and everything I ever did, I *am* sorry for. You act like you don't love me.

"Mir look at me," he pleaded.

Samira just turned on her heels and walked into the kitchen without saying a word. Having forgotten to turn off his cell phone, just as Ace was about to follow her, it vibrated; it was Nikki.

"Finally. Can you…" She couldn't even get out what she wanted to say because he abruptly cut her off. "Man, hit me back. I'm with my son," then he hung up on her.

Disgusted, Samira looked at him and said, "You ain't changed. You'll never change, no matter what. Please leave my house," she said, opening the kitchen door for him. With the stealth of a panther about to strike its prey, Ace rushed to the door and grabbed Samira by her neck with enough force to yank her kimar from her hair in the process.

"Look man, you keep testin' me. I'm not playin' with you," he said, hands still around her neck. She could feel her breath shortening and his revolver pressing against her. "Ali, let me go," she whimpered. He loosened his grip and she ran upstairs, locking herself in her room.

Ace walked upstairs and banged on the door. "Samira, open the door. She didn't open up fast enough, so he kicked the door right off the hinges.

"If you hit me I'm going to call the cops," she sobbed, terrified.

"I would never do that 'Mir, I love you too much to hurt you," he said, catching himself. "Yeah you love me; and her and her and her! I'm tired of it-just leave me alone! Someone else will love me and our son," she broke down and cried.

"What?" Ace yelled blinded with rage behind the idea of Samira loving someone else. He cocked his arm back to slap her when little Ali cried, "Daddy!" Ace turned to see his son standing in the doorway watching him. He simply turned and left the house, slamming the door on his way out.

Outside, Ace called his boy. He was really feeling the need to get away. "Rick where you at? It's about that time for us to bounce, meet me on CBW so I can give Kedar his whip."

"One," Rick acknowledged.

Ace got in Kedar's squatter and merged into the traffic on Newcastle Avenue. He rode in silence reflecting on what had just gone down with him and Samira, in front of his son. His cell phone danced across the seat and broke his thoughts.

"I need to get with you after nine," Black requested. "I might not be around, so I'll leave it with Keish," he said careful not to reveal that he and Rick were going out of town because then, everybody would feel the need to get away and business had to go on.

Detouring to Keisha's, Ace walked in and went straight to the kitchen. He pushed aside a worn panel of the drop-ceiling just above the refrigerator, reached his hand in the open space and felt around. He did not find what he was looking for at first, but there was no doubt in his mind that it was there. A second later he held in his hand his financial future. *Crack*.

The scale, sandwich bags and foil were kept in the drawer by the sink. Ace gathered up the tools of his trade. He bagged up a couple packages-four and a half ounces each, wrapped them in foil and put them in the freezer. Then he bagged the other fourteen grams, and put it in the butter dish compartment of the refrigerator. He put everything back where he kept it and locked up as he left. Before he got back in the car, he called Keisha and left her a message. "Hey babe-the meal you cooked was blazin'. I left some food in the freezer for the kids and what I couldn't eat off my plate, I left in the refrigerator."

He cruised down New Castle Avenue towards Southbridge, headed over to the East-side. As he sat for what seemed an eternity waiting for the light to change at the corner of Walnut Street, he found himself nodding with the boom-bap of some thunderous bass. He scanned the other stopped cars to see who had that sweet-ass sound system and his eyes fell on a Mercedes CL 600 in silver, dressed in Pirelli tires and twenty-two inch, three-piece AMG rims with chrome lips shining so bright they looked like somebody had licked them.

With his eyes traveling upward along the curves of the beautiful vessel, he noticed a sparkling bracelet dangling from a masculine arm. He also noticed that the arm belonged to Malik, and Little UC was in the passenger seat. The tint on the windows of Kedar's squatter was the perfect camouflage and had they not been stopped in front of the police station, the ambush would have happened right then and there. Ace anxiously massaged his heat. He turned right on Walnut Street when the car behind him beeped to alert him to the fact that the light had finally changed.

As he parked on Clifford Brown Walk, to watch his money flow, Kedar passed off to a fiend just as Ace cut the car off on 10th Street. He observed for a second, then strolled up the block to meet Rick. When he got close enough to be heard, he called to Kedar, "How you feelin' nigga? You act like you got shot five times."

"Man, I'm still a little sore, but you know mom-dukes is takin' care of me," said Kedar, sounding pitiful. "Holla at Keish if you get hungry," he announced as he passed by.
"Damn nigga, what took so long," Rick asked irritated while navigating his way to 495-North. "And where's your luggage?" "It's like Jadakiss said nigga, 'carry-on, no luggage; I'll shop when we get there," said Ace.

Rick shook his head. "Man, you are so wasteful."

Ace shrugged it off and asked what he felt was a more important question, "Where the weed at?" Rick passed him a sack and Ace looked at the bag. "All that time, why ain't you have it twisted already?"

Rick grinned and changed the subject. "What was wrong when you called earlier?" As Ace filled the cognac-flavored blunt with the moist, stem-free, seedless 'Purple Haze' buds, he confided in his boy.

" 'Mir be beefin' at the same dumb shit," as if he expected her to have accepted his reality by now. Rick cut his eyes at him and schooled him, "Do the right thing and leave them raggedy broad's alone. What happened?"

In his own defense, Ace said, "I do what I do out of love for her. She can't and won't do what Keisha does and she's not like Nikki...." His breath was cut short from the coughing spell induced by the long first drag of the blunt.

Rick laughed and said, "Nigga pass that over here," as he grabbed the blunt. "You can't handle the grown man buzz," he chuckled taking an even longer hit of the 'haze'.

When Ace got his wind back, he went on explaining, "Keish, that's my street wife, my down-ass bitch. She takes all the risks for me. Plus I smoke with her, drink with her, and get money with her. I got love for her, but she's a throw away. I'll never grow old with her," he accepted the blunt back. "Nikki the college jawn, man she's a boss freak! She got a tight ride, she's smart and her pussy is blaze. Bottom-line is, the sex game is the truth. As a matter of fact, let me hit her now!" he said grabbing his dick as they both laughed. "Samira," he continued, passing the blunt back to Rick, "That's my wife. I would do anything, even die for her. We will grow old together," he said with conviction.

Rick took in everything Ace had just said along with the intoxicating smoke and concluded, "Either I'm high or this shit almost makes sense." They laughed and got low with Young Buck all the way to the Philadelphia airport.

The car spiraled up to the fourth level of the parking

garage and came to a stop after circling a few times. Since they already wore the fragrance of Mary Jane, there was no need to give airport security reason to mess with them, so they shook the ashes off their clothes as they got out the car. It was a short distance to the elevators, so the two buddies agreed they wouldn't have a hard time finding the car when they came back. Getting off at the check-in level, even though the line was thankfully short, Ace still felt the need to drill Rick with the point he made earlier. "No luggage,and none of that checkin' in shit, either." Rick let that go because their flight was already boarding and they had to haul ass to gate C-16.

The staff made the last call for boarding when they got to the terminal. They wheezed out of breath. The roomy cushioned business-class seats were a welcome surprise, after the final sprint against the clock somewhere around gate B-20.

During take-off, Rick told Ace, that Mir really hooked them up. To which Ace responded, "See how everybody has a needed place?"

*Armani suits accent my Manolo Blahnik stilettos*
*As I step light*
*Keys to my Benz in my left, degree in my right*
*I am the greatest fear of a nigga who don't got it*
*No attachments*
*See I come and go as I please*
*From shopping sprees*
*To trips overseas*
*See I'm above average*
*Expensive meals, flawless diamonds*
*And fruitful conversation*
*Will have a brother stuck if he keep up*
*With history, Wall Street and public relations*
*The highlight of my life is sipping fine wine*
*While being pampered in a Jacuzzi*
*Some call me stuck up, but I prefer bourgeoisie*
*They say the ghetto is trifle but it's a state of mind*
*Where thugs hide, death lies and gunshots keep you alive*
*Where only the strong survive*
*So I heard, but opposites attract*
*Which led me to the slums; excited by the excitement,*
*Which gives me balance*
*In love with a man who uses drug dealing as his talent*
*Bourgeoisie, but*

## CAUGHT UP

"Man, we done been on several trips but this one was hot to death! That bitch I met at the hotel was bad!" said Ace, still hyped.

"No doubt," said Rick in total agreement. They found the car in the parking garage and headed back home. On the drive back, reality set in. "This trip really set me back. I need to regroup and get money," stated Rick, digging how much he actually spent.

"Man, you always cryin' broke. You don't even spend money. You probably got a million saved," Ace said. He was disgusted because Rick wasn't nearly as flashy as him, and he knew he didn't spend as much as he did either. He chirped Keisha since they were back on the money mission. He wanted to see if she had made any progress with UC.

"Where the hell is Keish?" he asked after getting no response from the chirp. He called her phone and got her voice mail. "Recently I've made some changes in my life, and if I don't call you back, you're one of 'em motherfucker."

"She's a crazy bitch," Ace laughed, "I guess she'll call me." Then he hit Samira and got her machine too. "Baby, I'm back in town. I wanted to see you so we can start our family life together. Just give me a chance. I love you. This is your husband Ace."

Since he was on a roll, he called Nikki. Of course, she made it her business to never miss his call, so she answered on the first ring. "Ace, where have you been?"

"Away on business, but I'm back in town now and I'ma come scoop you up later," he promised. "I miss you, Ace," she blushed.

"Do you? Well, you'll have enough time to show me how much later, but right now, I gotta go. I'll get with you.'Mir Simone and Nikki headed to McDonald's on the West-side to get a bite to eat. As they drove away from the drive-thru window, Simone spotted Terrence. "Damn, every time we come over this way, we spot your ass! What up brother?" Simone amused herself by clowning Terrence for a second. And when she was done, he looked at Nikki.

"What's up Nikki?" he said, as she munched down on the cheeseburger, as if it were her last.

Nikki barely looked up and grunted, "Stop playin' boy. You crazy." Then she went back to attacking the food again.

Simone checked how Nikki tore into the poor cheeseburger. "Bitch, you are not that hungry." Nikki paid her no mind as she zeroed in on the fries.

Simone continued to talk to Terrence in the parking lot. Nikki, on the other hand, went back into McDonald's for a chicken sandwich, which was just what she needed to wash down the burger and fries.

"When your girl gonna stop frontin' on me?" he asked. Simone let out a loud sigh. "Who knows? Go in there and buy her food, and maybe you'll get her attention that way."

He thought about it a moment, then strolled in, just as Nikki was handing her money to the cashier. He beat her to the punch.

"Big spender!" Nikki said. They both enjoyed a much needed laugh as Terrence passed the lady a five dollar bill.

"No disrespect intended, Nik, but you gettin' real fat," he said eyeing her mid-section. She rolled her eyes at him and grabbed her sandwich. She headed out the door with him right on her heels.

Back in Wilmington, Rick dropped Ace off at Samira's. He heard voices as he entered the house. Samira and Zulema were engaged in what looked to Ace to be a deep conversation.

"Salaam Alaikum," he greeted. "Who y'all talkin' about, me?"

"Yeah, like you're so important Ali," sassed Zulema.

Ace's face turned beet red, because he hated for anyone

besides his mom or Samira to call him by his given name.  He let it slide and turned to Samira, " 'Mir, why didn't you answer the phone?  Didn't you hear it?"  Without waiting for her excuse, he jogged up the stairs to unpack and shower before hitting the block to check on his money.

***

Keisha and Jasmine arrived back home in as much style as when they left.  The Hummer limo returned them to Keisha's from the airport.  They had been away for a weekend and were glad to be home.

"Damn!  That was fun!  Ain't nothin' like an all expense paid trip," said Keisha as she plopped down on her couch, dust flying everywhere.

"Damn, bitch, I'ma take a nap," Jasmine said feeling drowsy.  "And when I get up, we need to clean your house before we go out again," she called up to Keisha, who had run upstairs to see if the money from the mattress was gone.  She began straightening up her bedroom, she'd left in a mess.

Home for a little less than an hour, there was a banging at the door which awoke Jasmine, who had drifted off as soon as she sat on the couch.  She opened the door to find Rick standing there.  "Damn nigga, you ain't the cops," she said irritated.

"Where Keisha at?" he asked, ignoring her attitude.  "In my pocket nigga," Jazzy replied.

Getting nowhere with Jasmine, he hollered upstairs for Keisha as he landed on the first step.  "Where you been?" he questioned, seeing her busy at work in her room.

"What?  You ask a lotta' questions?  How was Miami?  You niggas, go there like you just goin' to a party around the way.  That's kinda' crazy since your ass is so tight, but you could chip in on Miami," she flipped it on him.

"Enough about that," he said unable to take the verbal

68

assault. "What's the verdict? You get that punk-ass nigga's code or what?"

"You know me, Keish with the fat ass gets what she wants. You and Ace need to come here later, 'cause I'm about to go to sleep," Keisha said to get rid of him. She showed him out without mentioning the details of her trip to Vegas. She finished cleaning her room and dozed off.

"Yo, this is Ace, who this?" Ace asked not recognizing the number on the caller ID. "Hi, it's Stacey. I just wanted to make sure you made it home safely."

Ace smiled from ear-to-ear at the sound of her sexy voice. "Thanks for askin'. I hope your flight was good too," he said sincerely.

"I'm glad you called. I wanted to know if I could take you out to dinner tomorrow night if you're free?"

"Hold on-let me check my schedule," she paused a moment,. "Just your luck. I am free tomorrow night. Call me in the afternoon and I'll give you directions to my place."

"Sounds like a plan," Ace confirmed as he pulled in front of Keisha's.

The first thing he noticed as he opened the door was how dark it was in the house. Once his eyes adjusted, he saw Jasmine stretched out on the couch. He headed upstairs in search of Keisha. He found her sound asleep on the bed.

"Yo Keish, get up. What's the verdict?" he started talking, disturbing her rest.

"What?" Keisha stirred, wiping the sleep out the corners of her eyes. She smiled at the sight of him. She missed him while she was away. Satisfied that she was fully awake, "Wanna get a quickie in?" he joked. "Nah nigga, you don't deserve the juicy fruit," she snapped. They both enjoyed a quick laugh when Keisha's phone rang.

"Hold up Ace, it's the boy," she said, shushing him. "Hey

baby," she answered sweetly.

"Hey-did you get enough rest?" asked UC.

"Of course, and thanks so much for the trip. I really enjoyed myself." She gamed him up. "That ain't nothin' compared to how it can be," bragged UC.

"Me and Amir are goin' to the 40/40 Club up New York. Wanna go?" She was fighting off Ace who by this time was fondling her. The attention she was giving UC was too much for him to witness.

"Hell yeah!" she said in spite of Ace's hands on her tits. "Can Jasmine go 'cause you know I don't leave the city without her?"

"Sure, I think her and Amir are vibin', so if you want her to go, then of course," said UC, now extending his invitation to Jasmine as well.

"What time you want me to be ready?" asked Keisha.

"Actually, I wanted you to come give me some of the juicy fruit before I make a few runs," said UC setting the booty call in motion.

"Alright, I'll be there in twenty minutes," she said, juices flowing. She got Ace out of her face by telling him she needed to go handle some business with UC real quick and then she awoke Jasmine again.

"Jazz," she hollered downstairs. "Drop me off at the boy's crib. Hurry up!" she said, totally caught up in the thrill of UC.

Ace, not to be gotten rid of that easily said, "I'ma be here handlin' some shit. I'll see you when you get back." Keisha barely heard him, because she was out the door so fast.

No sooner than she stepped in UC's door, they were at it hard. After a few hours of raw, hot sex, UC reminded Keisha that he had a few runs to take care of. Then he called Dominique while he strutted around getting his clothes ready.

She overheard him telling Dominique to meet him on

Bower Street as she lay there in his bed still tingling from the lovin'. Real big things are about to happen she smiled, as she tuned into the end of UC's conversation.

Once he hung up with Dominique, he walked over and slapped Keisha on the ass. The thongs made her ass shake like jelly. Staying only long enough to enjoy the jiggle, he was out.

The door barely shut behind him before Keisha was on the phone calling Ace. She got his voice mail on the first try but she tried again, awakening him on the second try.

"Yo, who this?" Ace answered, too groggy to see the caller ID.

"It's me nigga, get up! Where's Rick 'cause the boy is doin' a run right now on the North-side. He usually goes to Dominique's house first, then Khaliq's, so that's 28th Street then Bower Street," Keisha spilled just what he wanted to hear.

"Man look, that's what's up," Ace said pleased and now wide awake. "Does Dominique keep a burner?"

"Hell no, his punk ass acts tough, but he ain't got no burner. If you get a pen I'll give you the address. You can stake his house," Keisha said on the hush.

"Let me call Rick so we can set this shit off," Ace said with the taste of money on his tongue.

"Yo Rick, 28th, all black; the nigga, Dominique gonna be coppin' in a few. One,"

"One," Rick confirmed.

"Yo Keisha, good lookin' baby. Yo, don't be givin' that nigga too much of my ass. I don't want him to think it's his," Ace joked.

Keisha laughed, "There's enough ass for you daddy. We about to get paid, nigga. We 'bout to go to the 40/40 Club, I'll hit ya later."

Keisha continued to dress, slipping into her low-rider jeans and silk short-sleeve button-up blouse that UC had just bought her. She slid her feet in her new Manolo Blahnik's. She was feeling more upscale these days since she'd been seeing him. Admiring herself in the full-length mirror in UC's dressing room for one final inspection; she thought, *this ass done got me in a lot of places. I can get used to this.*

~*chirp*~ "Jazzy, we comin' to pick you up to go up New York, baby."

"Not tonight, I'm tired. Damn Bitch, we just got back from Vegas," Jasmine complained.

"So what, bitch? I ain't goin' up there alone. You complain' when we in the projects all day just chillin'; at least we ballin' now, bitch," Keisha convinced.

"Alright bitch, call me back," Jasmine said, surrendering to her friends persistence.

UC returned home after having been gone only twenty minutes just as she was heading out the bedroom, "Back so soon, babe?" Keisha asked bewildered.

"Yeah," said UC, "Mekhi will do the runs and Amir is waiting in the car. Is Jasmine going?"

"Hell yeah; we have to pick her up," Keisha said. Then, taking things in another direction, UC said, "Damn! You look good in those jeans." He got erect just from watching her butt in the tight denim. "Just think, you're all mine," he said, awaiting confirmation to boast his ego.

"Yeah, you know," Keisha obliged by grabbing his hand and placing it on her pussy, "This is all yours, baby, all you."

He enjoyed the moment with a grin, "Let's go. It's already eleven and it takes about two hours to get there." As UC set the alarm downstairs, Keisha watched. She already had one number in the code; now she had two of the four numbers. Not wanting to forget what she already knew, she punched the numbers into her cell phone.

Amir drove them to pick up Jasmine then they all hit the

highway laughing and talking the whole way. Keisha and Jasmine blew some herb and they all enjoyed some libation;this hot new vodka from Abstract Liquors. They stopped at a rest stop some-where in New Jersey, so that Jasmine could use the rest-room. "Babe let me use your phone, myservice is restricted out here," UC said. "These damn cell phones are crazy."

Keisha handed him her phone and got out the car to accompany Jasmine. UC wanted to call Mekhi to check that everything was going smoothly. Once he hung up from Mekhi, he scrolled through the recent calls; Ace's name showed up sev-eral times. One of those times was two minutes before they left for New York; there were also two digits before his name that looked
familiar. He just smiled and looked over at Amir then he dialed Dominique to check on the drop status.

Keisha and Jasmine came back from the rest room and got in the car. "You alright baby?" UC asked while leaning over to give her a kiss.

"Yeah, I'm straight," she answered. They pressed forward on the road to NYC; all of them getting in the party mood by 'leaning back with Fat Joe and the rest of the Terror Squad.

They arrived at the club in high spirits. As the valet parked the car, UC said to the ladies, "You girls go ahead in and mingle; we'll be in in a few minutes."

With Keisha and Jasmine inside, he called a few friends that were meeting him there and who were probably already inside. "Yo, what's up; we're here out front." A few minutes later a tall light-skinned brother with a long beard emerged from the club. He spotted UC and Amir and the three friends hugged. "So how you been, man?" the bearded brother asked UC.

"I'm chillin' man. I can't complain. I came with a female and I want to do that old respect test from back in the day. She's wearin' a pair of jeans with a fat ass, black heels and a silk button-up. She has a long ponytail, too," UC described.

"Cool," said the brother and they gave each other a pound as they headed into the club.

Amir and UC went straight to VIP to wait for the plan to be executed. Jasmine and Keisha, meanwhile, were at the bar,

"Can I get a apple martini?" asked Keisha..

"That'll be a Hennessey on the rocks for me," said Jasmine.

"I got the bill," said a brother from behind Keisha. She turned around and smiled. "Thanks, that was nice," she said.

"What's your name?" asked the brother, wasting no time.

"I'm Keish. What's yours?"

"I'm Bar Q," said the brother.

"What kind of name is that?" Keisha asked screwing up her face.

"You don't look like you're from NYC."

" 'Cause I'm not," said Keisha. "We from Delaware, nigga," Jasmine chimed in, high after only a few sips.

"You got a man, Ms. Delaware?" he asked Keisha.

"Look sweetie, a drink don't mean we fuckin' and yes, I got a man," she replied with an attitude.

"Damn baby. Why so hostile? I see you at the bar by yourself. The lucky man should have gotten your drink for you," Bar Q said indignantly. "And as far as fuckin' goes, no, I don't roll like that either. Excuse me bartender, set both these young ladies up, on me, all night."

Keisha smiled as Bar Q walked away. A few minutes later, UC appeared, "What's up babe? You enjoyin' yourself ?" he asked.

"Yeah, it's nice," she said. With that, he led her to the dance floor where they breathed, stretched, shook and let it all go, just as Reverend Mase preached. After having only been able to catch her breath for a minute while UC stepped off, over walked Bar Q.

"Hi, again, Ms. Delaware," he said.

"Damn, nigga, you don't give up, huh?" Keisha asked, clearly aggravated.

"Okay, we got off to a bad start. I'm Bar Q from Brooklyn and I just want to take you out sometime," he offered.

"Sorry Bar Q, thanks for the drinks, but I have a man," Keisha repeated.

He pulled out a crisp one-hundred dollar bill, wrote his number on it, and placed it on the bar; then he walked away.

"Bitch, you crazy!" exclaimed Jasmine. "UC ain't your man like that. You betta' take that nigga's number."

Keisha wasn't actually referring to UC when she mentioned her man. She was talking about Ace. "Ace's are wild, bitch. Don't you forget it," Keisha reminded Jasmine with all loyalty in place. Jasmine, however, paid her no mind because she was too busy eyeing the 'hundred dollar bill.

They partied like rock stars for the rest of the evening and just before they left the club, Bar Q called Little UC. "Man, your lady friend passed the test. She wouldn't even give me much conversation," he reported.

"Alright man, I'll be back up the way next week," said UC. With everybody back in the car, Keisha drove, so that everyone else could sleep.

***

Upon seeing Roy Jones get stretched across the canvas, unconscious for five minutes and finally carried out on a stretcher, Kedar and Black left the bar to go handle business. They eased up on Dominique walking his Rottweiler down the dark 28th Street alleyway and followed for a while. But as Dominique bent down to unleash the dog, Kedar came from behind and busted him in the head with a brick. Black swiftly quieted the barking dog, with a couple of .38 slugs. With no time to waste, "Grab the ya-yo," Kedar said. Black picked up the McDonald's bag lying next to Dominique. They laughed.

"Bingo," said Black checking the contents of the bag. "We got crack." They walked to Rash's deli, where they had parked the car earlier, adrenaline still rushing. Then they screeched from the parking lot, bumpin' corners all the way back to the East-side and Clifford Brown Walk. Mission accomplished, Kedar *chirped* Ace, "We got it."

"That's the shit. Meet me on the block," Ace responded.

Coming out of the store, Mekhi headed towards Dominique's house. He split his blunt down the middle as he walked up the block, nodding to the Schooly D ol' school joint Doc B had played earlier that was now stuck in his head, "*...some call it reefer/some call it weed/it's the thrilla'/it's the killa'/it's what I need/cheeba cheeba y'all....*" *Damn, that shit is catchy*, he thought, still bobbing to the music only he could hear. As he approached the alley between 27th and 28th, he saw a big mound in the street that he couldn't quite make out. As he got closer, the mound took the form of a person holding something that looked like a leash. Oh shit! His mind raced wildly standing over his slumped friend and his dog.

He couldn't tell whether Dominique was alive or not, but his dog, shot twice was not that lucky. Mekhi quickly checked Dominique's pockets before calling an ambulance. He also scanned the area for traces of the McDonald's bag. He must have put the work up, he hoped. Then he anonymously called 911.

"Yo, someone's been shot on Enterprise Street, between 27th and 28th-hurry!"

Mekhi left the scene and called UC, but the phone just rang before the voice-mail picked up, "I know it's late, but Dom just got hit! Call me back!" He hung up and fired up his blunt, taking in the first pull long and deep.

Meanwhile, Rick waited for Kedar and Black on the block to see how much they hit UC's crew for. The partners in crime arrived at the rendezvous point. They loaded two keys and a bird which was just enough to get them over the hump.

With the plans for dinner underway, and a couple more dollars in his pocket, Ace realized that he needed to go out incog-negro, so he called his Aunt Karin to see if he could borrow her Jeep Cherokee for his date with Stacey. "Yo, what's up Auntie?" he said cheerfully.

Knowing her nephew like a book, Aunt Karin got right to the point, "Yeah Ace-what do you want?"

"I'm gonna' need your Jeep tonight. I'll bring it back in the mornin'," he asked her confidently.

"Alright," said Aunt Karin, "But get it detailed before you bring it back."

"One," he said, grinning from ear-to-ear. Ace loved his dad's little sister. She always looked out for a brother.

Nikki called him while he was on his way to spend time with little Ali. He shot her straight to voice mail. *I'm not ready for her just yet,* he thought. Once he arrived at Samira's, it was all about him and his son. He spent a few hours of quality time with his baby boy, who was the highlight of not only his day, but of his life. And just being in Samira's presence, even for only a few hours, somehow soothed his soul. Samira, however, stayed in her room during his visit. She wasn't in the mood for him.

The flow was cut short when, *a ~chirp came through.* "Ali, my car will be at your mom's parked in the back and the keys will be in the mailbox," Aunt Karin instructed.

"Alright," he responded feeling irritated that the time with his son was coming to a close. On the flip-side, he was happy things were going as planned for the night. Although his heart was filled with love for his family; he kissed and hugged little Ali and sent him upstairs to his mom. Then he headed over to his mom's to get dressed.

It was a little known fact, but Ace knew how to get 'Dougie' when he needed to. Most people were used to seeing him in his street gear but he actually had impeccable taste and a great sense of style; a lesson learned from Samira's dad. He dressed in Ozwald Boateng silk and wool slacks and a linen shirt both in off white, and he topped it all off with a Jack Victor Italian worsted 100% cashmere sport coat. The thin red lines running through the classic black and crème pattern of the jacket, accented his golden complexion beautifully. He kept his jewelry to a minimum because he didn't want to come off too flashy, so he wore only a Tag Heuer timepiece and a solitaire two-carat diamond in his left ear.

After looking himself over in the mirror, he called Samira as he left the house. Once again, he got her machine. He left her a message declaring his love, strictly out of habit then he pointed the Jeep in the direction of the Delaware Memorial Bridge, Princeton bound.

The drive there was pretty boring until he got off at the Princeton/Lawrenceville exit. The manicured lawns, views of the lake and the majestic homes were breathtaking. *These niggas know how to live,* Ace thought.

Stacey wasn't sure what to expect from Ace tonight, but she was excited by the thrill of it all. Even though she was an extremely successful accountant, she just couldn't help her attraction to the thugs. She loved the mystery and the danger. The fact that he was fine as shit didn't hurt either. She had just slipped into her old stand by, her favorite Byron Lars black dress and was fastening the strap on her Etu Evans evening shoes when the doorbell rang. *And he's punctual too,* she thought glancing at the clock. She walked downstairs to open up the door for him. Upon opening the door she had to peel her bottom lip off the floor from the vision of the sexy man standing before her. *Damn!* she thought, I didn't know a thug could be that versatile.

She invited him in and showed him to her private lounge, which was in the cut, off the massive state-of-the-art kitchen. She offered him a seat. "May I get you something to drink before we go?"

"Sure, what you got?" he replied like everything was everything. He was really trying to concentrate on her to keep from looking around in amazement at her home.

"I've got some juice, water of course, and if you'd like something a little stronger." She pushed a button and a gorgeous painting he had been admiring slid back to reveal a full-service wet bar. "Help yourself and get comfortable. I'll be ready in a few minutes."

As she sashayed back through the kitchen, she was intoxicated by his trailing scent. He on the other hand, was confused by the wine selection, so he poured himself a glass of what he knew mostly from rap songs. *Moet.* As he sipped, he looked around and knew he had fallen into something special. Everything was the finest money could buy; the art, the marble, the crystal, the wood floors and the hand-woven rugs that covered them. It was sickening.

Stacey came downstairs completely put together and let Ace know she was ready. It was Ace's turn to pick up his lip when he feast his eyes upon her ample curves, which were beautifully draped by the flowing fabric of her stunning dress. She had to be the most thorough babe he had ever seen or kicked it with!

"I have reservations, babe, so let's go," Ace said. He made sure he opened the car door for her and extended his hand to help her step up. She could not help but notice the single rose which decorated the seat. She was impressed by the gesture and thought, *this little young boy has a nerve to be romantic.* The mellow voice of Kem provided the soundtrack on the ride to Ruth Chris' Steakhouse in Philly. Surprisingly, they had a stimulating conversation along the way and when the valet took the keys to park the car, Ace would not allow him to open her door; he was there to open it himself.

After an evening of good food, good wine, and good company Ace was not ready for things to end. "How about some more wine before I go?" he said with a sneaky smirk at Stacey's front door.

"Of course," Stacey said, not quite ready for the night to end either. She showed him to the den this time while thinking. *This little sexy brother just don't know; I will turn him out!* She poured him a cognac and cranberry before going upstairs to slip on her hoochie gear,some white booty shorts and a wife beater. She was back downstairs in no time, and found him sitting there looking rather delicious.

Stacey poured him another drink and stared at him with seduction in her eyes. Just looking at her made his dick rise. Unable to stand it any longer, she sat on his lap and said, "Ace, I had a real nice time tonight but you know how we can make it better?"

"Yeah," he said. "I know exactly how we can make it better." He took a big sip of his drink then put the glass down on the coffee table.

Gripping her by her hair just forcefully enough to excite her, he began to kiss her dribbling some of the drink in her mouth. He continued kissing her passionately until her chest heaved with anticipation of what was to come, then he picked her up and placed her gently on the plush, white rug right in the middle of the floor. She moaned as he softly sucked on and caressed her cantaloupe-sized breasts, flicking his tongue across her nipples. She squirmed beneath him as she got hotter, but she flipped the script on him by turning him over on his back to return the lovin'.

Sucking his dick until she felt him about to cum, she used her mouth to put on the condom, then mounted him, to take him for the ride of his life. His toes curled all the way up as she expertly massaged his dick with her juicy, wet pussy. Totally caught up in the essence of Stacey, he moaned, "Damn girl, where have you been all my life?" With the horse at full gallop, Stacey and Ace reached their heights hard and fast.

The night was just beginning though, and Ace was determined he was not going to let this old-head get the best of him. Stacey, being about eight years older than Ace, thought that if that was just the preview, she might have to keep him around for a while to see the entire movie.

He turned her over on her stomach intending to display all his star qualities. He licked her almost to the point of torture. His toungue slowly moved from her shoulders down to her ass. He lingered at her butt, circling her asshole with the tip of his tongue. At the same time, he slid his finger in and out of her, throwing her into a fit of ecstasy.

He knew he had her when she pushed his head further south, so he slid her legs open and blessed her pussy with his tongue, cooling all her heat with the dew-like moisture of his soft full lips.

*Damn*, she thought, *this young boy has got me open--wide open*. When she was swollen to his satisfaction, he entered her from the back and pounded her, with both his hands full of her ass. "Aaaaacccce, oh, Ace!" she screamed as she erupted in raw pleasure. It was the most intense orgasm she had ever experienced. "Damn Ace, give it to me baby...!"

He awoke beneath Egyptian cotton linens, not even remembering how and when he got to the bedroom. He was surrounded by light fluffy pillows. He felt as if he had awakened on a cloud. His stomach was thankful for the smell of food, but he needed to check his missed calls, since he had his phone off all night. It was still downstairs, so he got up and set out to find his way to the kitchen and then the den. There was a staircase at the end of the long hallway, and he decided to go that way. It spiraled directly to the kitchen and there he found breakfast and a note. It read:

Hey babe, you were sleeping like a prince so I decided not to wake you. Thanks for the exciting evening and hope you enjoy breakfast. Please set the alarm before you leave-

I created a code for you, 0516. Call me later,

Stacey.

*This babe is too much,* he thought as he took his plate to the breakfast room. He sat at the glass table and took in the beautiful view of her gardens. He watched the sculpted fountain peacefully spill water down its own walls. While he ate, he even tuned into the symphony the birds orchestrated. At that moment, he felt like a king.

Ace toured the mansion after filling his belly not really believing his eyes. "Damn, this is where it's at!" he said aloud.

There were eight bedrooms, each with private baths which was on the second floor, alone. He hadn't even gotten to the third floor yet, but he had plenty of time. She lives here alone in this big ass house. *This is going to be the perfect new spot,* he thought.

He found his way back to the master suite, dressed with a mile-wide grin. He pulled out his Nextel to check his missed calls. There were twenty-five, mostly from Nikki. He called her first and she picked up so fast, it made him lean back and shake his head.

"Ace?" she said, half surprised that he called her.

"Yes baby," he said sweetly.

"I want you to pick me up in front of Simone's in like forty-five minutes. We can talk then." Asking no questions about where he was and why he hadn't called, Nikki excitedly promised she would be there to meet him. He needed to cover his tracks on the home-front, so Samira was next on the return call list.

" 'Mir, I fell asleep at my Aunt Karin's. I'll be home later," he said trying to sound convincing.

"Whatever Ace," she replied nonchalantly. She was sick of him and his lies, so she didn't bother to ask any questions.

After returning a few more calls, Ace punched in his code to the alarm of Stacey's house and was out.

He took in all the sights on Alexander Road, making his way back to 295S out of the 'Golden Ghetto'.

***

Back in town, Ace parked the Jeep at Howard High to avoid the questions he was sure to get had he driven up in it. Nikki was sitting patiently in her Lexus as he strolled up on her, startling her with a sudden, "Hey baby!"

Nearly jumping out her skin, Nikki said, "Ace! That's not funny!" After the brief scare over, she then fired off a spray of 'wheres' and 'whys'.

"Where have you been? So if it's over between us, would you just tell me and stop stringin' me along?"

"Girl, stop talkin' stupid," he kissed her to calm her down.

"Mmm-Hmm," Simone said from the door as she observed the player working his magic on her girl.

"Whatever, you hater," he said grabbing his crotch in her

direction.

"Babe, can we talk now?" begged Nikki.

"Later, I promise," he said putting her off for the ump-teenth time. "I'ma scoop you up later."

Visibly pissed, Nikki peeled off Clifford Brown Walk, leaving skid marks. She hit the off key to her phone. Ace walked up the block, not affected in the least by Nikki's road show. He curled his upper lip to catch the scent of Stacey.

Headed to play a couple dollars on the crap game with Rick and Black, he hadn't even gotten all the way up the street before his phone vibrated. He looked at the number and smiled. "Hey babe-what up? Happy to hear your voice," he said.

"Hey yourself," she said. "I miss you."

"I just seen you this mornin' babe," he said, tongue full of honey.

"I know, suga' but last night makes me want to see you more or should I say more of you," she played.

"Woman you better stop spoilin' me like this. Don't start nothin' you can't finish," he warned.

"I'm a grown woman and I finish everything I start," she laughed. "I was calling to see how you liked breakfast and to let you know that I'm getting ready for a business conference in Atlanta, so I probably won't see you before I go. My car needs a detail so if you wouldn't mind taking care of that before I get back, I'd appreciate it. Since you have a code now, let yourself in to get the key and don't forget to reset the alarm when you leave."

"Anything for you. Hit me up when you get off your return flight," he said recalling how the pink flower between her legs bloomed all night. "I can still taste you on my lips."

"Boy, you crazy!" she giggled recalling how downright diabolical he was with his tongue. "I have a meeting to go to now, I'll call you later," she said, disappointed that they couldn't get in a quick phone sex session.

Rick noticed Ace cheesin' that whole conversation and curiosity got the best of him. "What you so happy about nigga? We hit the lotto or somethin'?"

"Naa nigga; that chick from Miami is a winner-believe that!"

"Man, the bitches'll be the death of a nigga. Ain't your plate already full?" Rick asked amazed that Ace could squeeze in somebody else.

Adjusting his pant leg to relieve the pressure of his hard-on, he replied, "Man she's bad, nigga, a boss freak!"

They hung out on the block awhile, joking and laughing.

"The Lounge is havin' somethin' tonight and we in there, nigga," Rick said.

"I heard that," said Ace. "I gotta get my aunt's car detailed, so let's take a ride to Scrub-a-Dub." They walked down CBW, in the cut, and got in the Jeep.

Half way to the 'Dub', Ace's phone vibrated. Nikki couldn't resist calling him again. "What man, what?" he answered, aggravated by the lack of breathing room.

"Look Ace," said Nikki, disgusted and tired of chasing him. "I'm tired of you ducking me and playing games. Just don't call me anymore. I'll handle things myself."

"Look babe, a lot of things have been goin' on tonight. I'll be by to pick you up, I promise." His soft tone got to her. "Okay Ace, but you promised," she whined.

Rick just stood by and watched his boy work his magic. "Boy you crazy. I guess you a pimp by blood not relation', huh?" They slapped hands and laughed real hard.

Ace picked Nikki up in Stacey's Mercedes. "Now what's wrong?" asked Ace, frustrated by her ugly expression.

"Look Ace, I've left several messages telling you that I'm pregnant and I don't know whether I want to have an abortion," Nikki said. "So if you don't want to be a part of this situation, I'll understand." She began crying uncontrollably.

Ace wiped her tears. "Right now is not the time for a baby, but it's your decision. I love you girl."

Totally snapping Nikki yelled, "You love me? I don't know shit about you, Ace! Where do you live? Can I meet your son, your mother? What is it with you?"

"Enough," Ace calmly interrupted. "You want to know where I live, let's go." He steered the '350 to the Delaware Memorial Bridge headed towards Princeton, NJ.

Nikki looked in amazement as the big beautiful home came into full view as they pulled into the winding driveway. He disabled the alarm immediately upon entering and Nikki thought excitedly, *Damn, I knew he was ballin'- but not like this; my baby will be set!*

"Would you like some juice or water?" offered Ace. "Naa," said Nikki. "But where is the bedroom? Let me look around," she said giddy.

"Baby, come here," Ace said seductively.

As she stared into his deep onyx eyes, they undressed each other right where they stood. "I really missed you, babe, really I did," said Nikki. Ace made love to her, there on the living room floor. For round two he carried her up the stairs.

After a few hours of quieting her with the strength of his stroke, he turned to Nikki, "Babe listen, I have a lot of business to take care of, so lay here and get some rest till I get back. Don't leave this room, I'll be back later." He kissed her on the forehead and shut the door of the bedroom suite on his way out. Between the lovemaking session and her unborn child, Nikki was exhausted. She dozed off under the sheets.

Ace started up the Mercedes and cranked up the volume. Tupac blasted through his speakers, "*...all I need in this life of sin/is me and my girlfriend/down to ride to the bloody end/is me* *and my girlfriend. ..."* He exited the highway at Twelfth Street headed towards 'The Lounge' to chill and watch the replay of the Roy Jones fight.

When he parked, he noticed Terrence's BMW and Little UC's Hummer in the parking lot. *What the hell is going on?* he thought. Spice met him at the door, "Yo Ace, there are different sets in here tonight. Everyone is chillin', watchin' the fight, so no dumb shit alright?"

Everyone always agreed to chill because of the respect they had for the old head, Spice. "Cool with me," Ace smiled more at ease.

He entered the place giving everyone dap. They all whooped and hollered watching Roy get knocked out. And it was no less brutal the second time around. "Damn!!" hollered UC, "I had a couple dollars on that boy!"

Then for no apparent reason, UC *chirped Keisha,* "Keisha, babe, you at the crib waitin' for me right?" he spoke into his Nextel loud enough for those within ear shot to hear. He had a smile that would have lit up the room had the lights not already been on.

"Yeah, see you when you get in. Your kitty cat is waiting for you," she purred having no idea who he was around.

"Look at this boy, Rick. Suckers do what they can but players do what they want," commented Ace.

Sensing a beef cooking, Spice gestured for the dancers to come off-stage. The men readied for battle. Little UC and his crew; Amir, Khaliq and Mekhi opted to head for the door. On the way out, Amir made it a point to stare down Ace. Ace communicated with his eyes only. You don't want it.

Spice watched as Amir and Ace walked towards each other and quickly jumped between them. "Here fellas, y'all want some candy?" he asked pushing one of his girls in their faces.

"Naa, I'm out," Amir said keeping his gaze fixed on Ace

and without giving the nearly naked woman a second glance. "But a nigga know where I be at, North-side nigga.," then he was gone. Face his trademark shade of red, Ace said through gritted teeth. "Man, that bitch Keisha has to hurry up and get that code. I want this nigga so bad!"

"Calm down, man. Keisha never failed us before. She knows what she's doing. The patient one gets the bait," Rick said keeping Ace focused. "The strip party started anyway, so let's have some fun man."

Not feeling it, Ace went into the office of The Lounge and fell asleep on the couch.

Nikki woke up without Ace next to her, so she went to the bathroom and washed up. After she got dressed, she snooped around the house to get some clues about Ace, the mystery man.

*It took him long enough to bring me here. I want to savor the moment,* she thought as she left the master suite eager to explore. She called Simone to report, "Hey girl, guess where I am? Out New Jersey, at Ace's house! This shit is really hot. So far I've counted eight bedrooms, all with private bathrooms and...." The piercing shrill of the alarm going off cut her news flash real short.

"Oh shit Simone, the alarm is going off, I'll call you back!" Nikki rushed downstairs and listened as a voice asked Ms. Lockett if she were okay and if there was an intruder. Panicked, she called Ace and left him a frantic message before responding to the questions coming through the alarm speaker. "I'm just a visitor and who is Ms. Lockett?" asked Nikki.

"What is your name? Are you okay? Do you know the code? Where's Ms. Lockett? An officer will arrive in a few minutes, but don't worry, that's just normal procedure," the gentleman's voice assured.

Nikki called Simone back to ask if she would come get her. "Bitch, I ain't drivin' all the way to Princeton! Where the hell is that nigga, Ace?"

Ignoring her objections, Nikki mapped the plan. "I saw a place called the Nassau Inn, on Nassau Street, that we drove past before we turned to get to the house. I'm gonna' start walkin'," Nikki said shaking. Hearing that the fear in her voice was real, Simone told Nikki she was on her way and she also stayed on the phone with her while Nikki walked.

\*\*\*

It was 11:30am, the following day when Ace and Rick awoke. They were still in the backroom office of 'The Lounge'. The first thing he did was turn on his phone, just in time to receive Stacey's call. "Hi sweetie, I'm on the plane about to take off. Something is wrong at the house. The police just called and said someone tried to break in and that they were still in the house when the alarm went off." Concern was deep in her voice.

Remembering that he'd left Nikki in the house, he said, "I'm on my way there now, baby, don't worry. There's no need for you to rush home, I'll take care of everything."

"I'm on the plane already and I've been calling you all morning, so I'll see you when I get home," said Stacey.

Ace raced for Princeton but by the time he got there, the cops were already there writing up their report. "Excuse me sir, who are you?" asked the officer.

"Ms. Lockett sent me to check on everything. I'm a good friend of hers," Ace said, trying not to sound as paranoid as he felt.

"Oh," said the officer, looking Ace dead in his eyes. "Well it doesn't look as though anything is out of place."

"Alright," said Ace politely. "Thanks a lot officer. I'll go call Ms. Lockett now."

He spread his wings and flew around the house straightening up. He made up the bed and threw the dirty linens in the washer to start. A few hours later, Stacey walked in practically breathless, "What happened? Is anything missing?"

"Naa babe," Ace said calmly. "Nothing is missing and I cleaned up. I'm about to bounce, though, I have to take care of some business in the city. I'll be back later." He kissed her on her forehead then he left.

Stacey took off her shoes and checked her house. In the living room, the foot of her pantyhose got stuck on a particular spot and she wondered what had gotten on her rug. She got the rug cleaner and began working on the stickiness, fondly remembering how she and Ace had made love in that very place before, with no covers. She could have sworn she'd done a better job of cleaning it up.

*Maybe he spilled something*, her thoughts drifted as she scrubbed and checked around to see that everything in that room was accounted for.

***

Ace tried calling Nikki while he drove home, but got no answer. He left a message, "Yo, it's Ace. Where you at and why did you leave my house like that?"

When he arrived on CBW, Simone was in the doorway, as usual. "What, no work today?" Ace inquired.

"Naa, I had to pick my girl up in the wee hours of the mornin'."

"That was some crazy shit too Ace," Simone scolded. "And when did you move to Jersey. I didn't know you were ballin' like that-damn nigga?"

"Don't be runnin' your mouth about my business, either. Where's your girl at?" he asked.

"I took her home so she could get ready for work. That was really some crazy shit," she reiterated.

"Why did she leave my crib like that?" he asked.

" 'Cause they were callin' for some woman through the speaker on the alarm." Simone took too much pleasure in telling him.

"Man, that was my accountant. What you got to drink?" Ace asked as his nerves still rattled from the morning action. "Yo, let's light somethin', Simone," he suggested.

"Nigga, I only smoke cigarettes, but you can blaze here if you want," she said playing the happy hostess.

Ace plopped himself on her couch, laid back, lit his blunt and sipped on the Corona Simone had just handed him. "It's still early and Court TV is on. That shit is funny," said Simone.

Ace stared at her, sizing her up and licking his lips. "Yo 'Mone, your ass is faaaaaaatttt."

"Boy, you trippin'."

"Naa, for real, your ass is faaattt. Get up and go get me another beer," he requested. Simone giggled as she jiggled her way to the kitchen. She switched as hard as she could on her way to the refrigerator. "Here," she said, handing him the beer, "I think you're drinkin' this Corona way too early and way too fast."

"Damn! I like how you fittin' in them jeans," he said ignoring her comment. She smiled and sat on the floor to smoke a cigarette. Ace asked her to come to him.

"What? I can hear you from here," she said, not wanting it to be easy for him.

"I'll come to you then," he said as he slid to the floor next to her. "Let me hit that cigarette."

Simone passed it to him. He smiled and put it out. Simone laughed and turned back to watch tv. Ace started massaging her neck, which nearly sent her up the wall. It felt so good. Then he began to fondle her breasts. She played like she wanted to resist by half-heartedly pushing him away but the slight smile on her face told the true story. "What are you doin', man, we can't do this?" she expressed with her mouth while her hand caressing his balls, told a different version.

Surprised by his generous proportion, she licked her lips. "Yo, let me smoke this L," he fell back with a devilish grin. He took his pants off and sat on the couch to spark. Simone played between his legs while he smoked, arousing him to new heights. Ace pushed her head down and she put up no resistance. She licked and sucked on his manhood as if she had always wanted it.

*Dirty bitch*, he thought. He made no sound as he shot off all over her face, still inhaling and exhaling the intoxicating smoke. She knew it must have felt really good to him as hard as he came. Ace smiled and put on his pants as if nothing happened. "You'll always have the fattest ass," he said.

"Ace, we ain't fuckin'," Simone said, angrily wiping her face on her sleeve. "Oh? I'll be back for that ass later," he gassed her up, but he actually didn't want to hit that. He had pretty much gotten what he wanted. He left Simone's and walked to Kedar's house.

"Hey, Kedar!" Ace called from outside. Kedar's mom came to the door to let him in. "Good afternoon, Ace."

"Hi Mrs. Wilmore, may I use your bathroom?"

"You know where it is honey," she said stepping aside to let him in. Ace went to the bathroom where he washed his penis off with alcohol. He thought that would kill the stench of oral sex and any germs he may have picked up.

"Yo Ace, where you comin' from?" Kedar asked, as he emerged from the bathroom.

"From seein' if Nik was at the babe, Simone's house," he said.

"Yeah? I heard that," Kedar said with a smirk.

Sitting in the park on 24th Street, UC and Amir half-way watched the basketball game being played. Cianni walked up to UC smiling.

"Hey UC, I see you like low life bitches. Ill, that smut Keisha is drivin' your whip," she taunted.

UC responded with all seriousness. "What? It don't matter if you a dime, a smut or a bitch." Then he walked away because he had an appointment to have the disc changer fixed in the Hummer. He couldn't wait either. The radio got on his nerves, because he was in the business. Regardless, he flipped through the radio stations several times before settling on Power99 and the *Wendy Williams Experience.*

# CHAPTER 6

## Five Minutes

It was getting really late, as Samira cooked dinner. She waited for Ace to bring the spaghetti sauce. She called him to see what could possibly be taking so long. The voice mail picked up on the first ring as was normal these days.

Now second nature, she punched in his code, even though she promised herself that she wouldn't do it anymore. Just like she thought, she heard that bitch Keisha's voice, "Yo nigga, it's me. Hit me up-I got some news for ya." Samira erased that irritating ass message.

The next message was from some woman named Stacey. "Hey babe, it's Stacey. I just wanted to thank you for dinner. I had the nicest time ever! Call me." Samira sucked her teeth and erased that message, too.

Her heart dropped, as did the phone, the moment she heard the key turn in the front door. Ace waltzed through the door, all happy with a dozen roses, a gift bag and the sauce. Heading straight to the kitchen with an extra spring in his step, he leaned over to kiss her on the forehead.

"What's up 'Mir?" Ace could tell by the look on Samira's face that something was wrong. He also knew that she wouldn't say anything either. She had been through so much with him in the past years, as well as in the present, that there was truly nothing left to say. Nothing she could say would change his trickin' ass, but her eyes told the story her mouth couldn't.

Samira went back to preparing dinner and Ace simply stared at her from where he sat at the kitchen table. "How was your day, ?" he asked.

"Fine, and yours?" she replied pleasantly,but sternly.

"Well, you know the game is the same. Some days are slower than others," he went on, as he pulled out his half-ass player's knot and began counting. "Babe I got a surprise for you," he said getting up to hand her the bag from Saks. She stopped stirring her sauce to open the bag. It was a Chanel scarf and matching handbag.

"Thanks," said Samira, quite unimpressed. She put the bag on the table and went back to her sauce.

"Nothing but the best for my 'Mir," Ace boasted, reaching to kiss her. She turned away not really feelin' him at all.

"What's wrong now? What did I do now?" he asked, actually sounding wounded.

"Nothing," Samira said flatly. "Thanks for the gift, again." She turned away and went back to cooking. He could no longer dazzle her with the flash and the floss. She had been seeing it for years and it had definitely worn thin.

*The best gift ever, would be for him to quit playing in these streets and to return to the lessons my father taught him*, she thought. She let out a little giggle to keep from crying.

Ace looked up from counting his money, " 'Mir, what's funny?"

"You," she answered. "And you're right, the game don't change. When will you?"

"I'ma ball till I fall," he announced.

"Oh, you'll fall alright," she promised.

Ace's phone vibrated. He had forgotten to turn it off before coming in the house. It was Nikki. *Damn, this bitch be stalkin'*, Ace thought. He did not answer. He sent her call to voice mail. Then he turned back to Samira. "You need some help, 'Mir?" he offered.

"No thanks," said Samira. She paid him no mind as he sat

and stared at her, nor did she turn around to face him. She was so tired from the past thirteen years and all his bullshit, she knew her silence would hurt him more than anything she could say.

Ace lingered half the night. They ate dinner as a family and he gave Ali his bath. Samira cleaned up the kitchen then went straight to her bedroom. Ace came in the room once he tucked in Ali. "Hey, can I get some?" he had the nerve to ask.

"You can get some advice, nigga-that's about it," she said seriously.

"What? You fuckin' somebody else?" he asked face turning red with the thought of someone else enjoying her delicious fruits.

Samira looked him the face, kissed him on the lips, and said, "No." Again, her eyes told the whole story.

She went to Ali's room to check on him before lights out. Ace followed. " 'Mir, you know I love you girl..." Hearing it all before, she cut him off.

"Yeah, yeah, I know you love me and them," she added.

"Who is them?" he asked. "Man, you're crazy, it's only you," he tried to sound offended.

"If you really think that I believe that then you're the crazy one," she shot back. "Nothing makes me that special to you. Oh, maybe our son, but you're still the same old Ali or Ace or whatever they call you," she said, clearly hurt.

"Man look, I don't want to argue. Just know that I love you." He kissed little Ali and said, "Tell mommy we love her," as she walked out. He fell asleep in his son's bedroom on the floor.

Samira burned inside, because she really wanted to say something about the messages that she'd heard. Her pride would not let her. Plus, all he would do is lie anyway.

In her room, she asked herself when she was going to be done with all his bullshit. As the tears began to flow, she buried her face in her pillow, to silence the sobs until sleep finally rescued her.

\*\*\*

Keisha was on her way to the mall, when she noticed the time. "Damn, it's 3:30," she said, quickly turning on the radio for her favorite radio talk show, *The Wendy Williams Experience*. Today's topic was accepting the fact that you're the other woman. *I should call up there and get me some advice*, Keisha pondered. *Things is gettin' crazy.* She found a parking spot and dialed the number. It was fifteen minutes on the redial button before her call was answered.

"Yo Wendy, this is K from the 'Bridge in Delaware. Listen Wendy, I been dealin' with this nigga for like eight years and I have two kids by him. He's a dealer and he put me up to set up another nigga. But at the same time, this new nigga is passin' off like crazy. I was supposed to have been got the info to rob him but shit is too sweet. What should I do?"

"Girl, are you crazy?" Wendy asked. "Aren't you scared for your life? Who is this dude your husband or something?"

"Naa, we get money together and we ain't married," Keisha reported. After giving Keisha some advice, they hung up. Apparently, Keisha made a lasting impression because Ms. Williams continued talking about her on air.

"You young girls are crazy! She's got two kids by this man and no ring, no commitment and she's putting her life on the line for him. I guess that's what they mean when they say 'ride or die bitch'. Giirrrl, he don't love you. Run for cover..." as laughs echoed the station.

Keisha turned off the radio and hustled inside to get her sneakers. While she was at Lady Footlocker, Ace called. "Yo, how's my number one bitch?"

"Nigga, you crazy. I'm at the mall gettin' a pair of

sneaks," Keisha replied.

"Damn! That nigga keep you tight! What he tryin' to wife you? Don't make me have to shoot that nigga," Ace joked.

"You crazy! So far I found out that you and him cop from the same cat, Malik, from Philly, but Malik be givin' this nigga deals like crazy. He picks up every Thursday at the McDonald's on Broad and Girard. The one they call 'Club McDonald's'. We went a few days ago," Keisha gave up all that she knew.

"Good lookin'. I been dealin' with Malik for a while and I thought UC must be dealin' with him too by the shit he knows about Wilmington. Let me hit you back and get them codes so we can come up. This nigga can't keep ballin'," Ace said all hyped up by the progress."

He immediately chirped Rick. "Yo, let's shoot up Philly tonight for the game. The Sixers are playin' the Raptors. Maybe I can holla at the boy Malik, 'cause he got season floor seats. We need to talk to him about doin' more business with us."

## Shahida T. Fennell

*Headstrong, let him pop that*

*Desires lustful*

*All you heard is 'I like that'*

*Legs back, damn I felt that*

*Don't know for sure the exact*

*But I know by the blow and the expression*

*The release was explosive*

*Now 270 days of pain came*

*All from five minutes of pleasure*

*Got me shivering*

*The stress from something precious*

*God bless this but*

*You took advantage of my weakness*

*Heated sex, attention and sweetness*

*Was your trap*

*Now instead of late night cuddles and weekend trips*

*My book bag is filled with diapers, wipes, milk and shit*

*Five minutes, ain't that something*

## FIVE MINUTES OF PLEASURE

Ace sat in the car, still outside Samira's house, and rolled a blunt. He scrolled his missed calls list and noticed that Keisha, Nikki and Stacey had called several times. He continued rolling his blunt and put on his Jack Frost CD. Good weed and good music put him in a chill mode. He lit his blunt and pulled off, headed towards Newcastle Avenue.

~*chirp*~ "Keisha, what up? Jack got me really thinkin' about you," he said, drawing her in.

"What? Who the hell is Jack?" she asked, baffled. "Jack Frost, his new mix CD is butter *'...gutter bitch/it's you/it really is, oooooo...'*" Ace attempted to flow in between blunt hits.

"Fuck you nigga. Come through real quick. I got news for 'ya," she went on all business.

"I'm on my way baby." Knowing that Keisha would be a long minute at the mall, Ace rode through the East-side.

"Simone!" he called as he honked the horn outside her house. She rushed to the door, all teeth.

"What up, Ace? Nik, ain't here."

"I ain't blowin' for her," he said. "How's that fat ass?"

She smiled, "Why you ask? You ain't want it. What you scared, nigga?"

"Yeah alright," he said. "Come to the car right quick. I need you to do me a favor." She leaned over in the window and he stuck his tongue in her ear and whispered, "Look-Rick needs somewhere to put that shit, so I'ma tell him to give it to you. Is it cool?"

"Of course," she said feeling him. "But don't tell Nikki."

"See how my tongue felt in your ear? That's how it will feel once I hit it," he said as he pulled off. An evil grin crept across his lips as he rode up the block to bullshit with Rick and Black.

"Ace's up-deuces down, niggas!" Pitch the quarter was in full swing on the corner of the block.

"Ace, let me hit that," said Rick.

"Naa, nigga; puff- puff- keep is the rotation on this one. But come here though."

Rick walked over to where Ace stood. "Move that shit out of the spot and take it to Simone's." Rick's eyes got real big before he asked, "Simone's? How you pull that one off?"

"Let's just say that she's on my dick. Let me go meet Keish. I'll call you later. One."

He was still indulging in the herbal essence when he parked in front of Keisha's. He saw Khaliq grinding in the cut.

"Yo, what up, Khaliq?"

"My main man, Ace," said Khaliq, hand extended. After exchanging hand shakes, Ace walked into Keisha's house screaming for her as he always did.

"You don't have to holler nigga, I'm right here," said Keisha, from the couch where she sat twisting a blunt of her own.

"You lookin' good," said Ace, rubbing himself. He thought about how he hadn't sexed her for a minute, especially since she'd been on her mission.

"Yeah nigga, a bitch feelin' good too," she said beaming.

"What's the verdict?" asked Ace, now all business.

"He's supposed to be meetin' the boy Malik again which means he must be about to score big, real b…"

The light knock at the door and the door opening ended her report, mid-sentence. The surprised look on her face instantly made Ace turn around. It was Little UC.

"Keish, you ready?" UC asked her looking from her to Ace.

"Yeah, let me holla at my baby dad, right quick," she said, playing things off.

"Alright, but hurry up. We got to go, so I'll be out front," he said, his gaze resting on Ace. They looked each other up and down until UC spoke, "What's up?"

"Bitches and money," said Ace.

"I heard that," said UC. Then back to Keisha, he said, "Babe, put them Prada sneaks on that I just bought you," he said, eyeballing Ace. Keisha, still in the habit of wearing Air Ones with everything, ran back upstairs to change remembering her new options.

"Alright," said Ace returning UC's glare, "I'll go to your mother's and check on the kids."

"Whatever," Keisha called downstairs.

As Ace walked to his car which was parked in front of UC's, he noticed Amir talking to Khaliq. "Damn, that bitch's pussy must really be the bomb! Your man and that nigga be comin' and goin' one after the other," observed Khaliq.

"Word," said Amir. "Maybe she is the bomb," he said loud enough for Ace to hear.

Ace gave him a look that would have killed him if eyes alone could kill. "UC, man, come on! We about to hit Dave and Busters, tell that bitch to hurry up!" said Ami. UC came out and walked towards Amir smiling and nodding.

\*\*\*

On the caller ID, a Jersey number appeared as the phone rang. Samira thought about how those damn bill collectors will call your house any time of day or night, so she let the phone just ring.

# CHAPTER 7

## C. O. W. Casualties of War

"Speak to me," Keisha said, picking up the phone on the first ring.

"It's me, who else be callin' you?"

"Nobody. Only you, baby," she blushed, instantly aroused by the voice on the other end.

Rick said nothing as he sat on the couch watching Keisha slip on the jeans she had on the night before. She grabbed her jacket and headed for the door. "Where you goin' at?" asked Rick, seeing her huge smile.

"Why nigga. You ain't my man!" she snapped.

"That's why I ain't your man, 'cause you always up to somethin'," he shot back.

"Fuck you," she said and ran out of the front door. As soon the door shut, Rick walked over to the window. He watched, puzzled, as Keisha got into the black Pontiac Bonneville sedan. The windows were tinted, so he couldn't make out the driver. *Damn, who the hell is that? This girl knows more niggas,* he thought, returning to his spot on the couch.

"Hey babe," Keisha said leaning over to give her suga' some suga'.

"Relax," he said, "put your seat belt on."

"Where we goin'?" she asked.

"Shopping. What you think?" he questioned.

"Damn! What did I do to deserve this shopping spree?" she asked excited, as the car pulled out of the projects and onto 495-North. They rode in silence while he focused on the highway. Keisha rubbed his bulge for a little ways before unzipping his pants. He sat nearly motionless, concentrating on the road, while Keisha slurped and sucked his dick for miles. She paid it no mind when the car stopped. *Damn, they said my head shot was like that, but I ain't never had a nigga stop the car behind it feelin'* so *good*, she thought, proud of her skills.

She lifted her head and asked, "Why we stop so soon?" as if she didn't know.

"You know what I've learned in the game?"

"No nigga. What have you learned in the game?" she played along.

"Never get involved with nothin' you can't leave in sixty seconds," he continued.

"Okay, now I think you been watchin' too many gangster movies, nigga," she chuckled.

"You must have thought I was a sucker," he said, indignantly. "You can't play a player," he calmly said.

Keisha snapped, irritated that he killed the sexy vibe they were on. "Fuck you nigga! All that shit I don't hear about is what fucks the deal! What? I ain't suck your dick right?"

"You still don't get it, you dumb bitch?" he asked with a smirk. "Every move you made, I put in place. I treated you like a dime even though you were a trick."

"Whatever," she sucked her teeth, rolled her eyes and leaned back. *This nigga love to hear himself talk,* she thought. He preached on, "Bitch, I gave you a rope made of diamonds and you still chose to hang yourself."

Keisha thought about when she first met Ace and how he was the sharpest guy in school. She also thought about her son Richard and the first time he took a step. She let out a little giggle thinking about how crazy Jazzy was and reminisced on the high times they had with UC and his crew. The phone calls, the codes, setting up Dominique.....

Two shots to the dome. She lay slumped over with blood oozing from the side of her face and cum still around her lips. The door opened and her lifeless body fell to the pavement after being pushed out as if emptying the car of trash from the floor. Before he pulled off, he made a quick call.

"Yo cuz-o, shit been done. A bitch is a bitch and a trick is a trick. You had to get her before she got you. Now what we gonna do about her bitch-ass boyfriend?"

"Man for real, that nigga don't want work. He ain't ready for us. Let's play it by ear." The car slowly merged into traffic, back towards Wilmington.

Keisha really never thought about karma. She never realized how all your deeds will return to you with the same intentions with which you performed them. Her body wasn't discovered for an entire day.

Jasmine walked into Keisha's place asking Rick where she was.

"Man, I don't know. She ain't with you?" he asked. They heard honking outside and went to the door to see UC, hollering for Keisha.

"Yo Keish! Come on baby. We gotta roll!"

Jasmine responded, "Hey U, she ain't here. We still goin' to the mall?"

"Yeah, come on."

As Jasmine jumped in the Hummer, UC handed her a blunt. "Spark this 'L' while I hit my girl on her cell." *~chirp~* "Yo Keisha.." No response. UC grinned Rick's way and pulled off.

*Sucka' ass nigga,* thought Rick observing the whole scene.

*~chirp~* UC tried Keisha again. "Keish, where you at?" Once more, no response.

\*\*\*

107

"News flash- a young, African-American female was found dead on the pavement in Chester," the news reporter said. "The police called it homicide and wanted help with identifying her. The only clue was a tattoo on her back that read, 'Ace's are wild' with all four aces fanned out." They showed a picture of Keisha's back. Samira's mouth dropped as she listened in disbelief. Although she did not like the fact that she and Keisha shared the love of the same man, she was concerned enough to immediately call Ace.

"Yo, who this?" he spit into the phone.

"It's 'Mir. I think you need to get up. That chick Keisha was found dead in Chester last night."

"Mir, you trippin'. I'll hit you back," he said, not really comprehending what he was just told. He turned to Rick, "Yo Rick, get the fuck up. 'Mir just called saying that she thinks Keish is dead."

Just then, there was a thunderous knock at the door. Jasmine fell in screaming and hollering, "Somebody killed Keish, y'all! Ace, she's dead, she's dead!" She collapsed in Rick's arms.

Ace sat emotionless; it still hadn't sunk in for him. "Man, y'all buggin'. Call that nigga UC and see if she's with him."

"I was with UC and Amir all night and Keisha never answered our calls. I figured she was with you," Jasmine sobbed.

"I haven't seen her all night," said Ace, still not believing.

They all left Keisha's apartment and got into Rick's car with Ace behind the wheel.

"The last time I seen her was yesterday mornin'. She got a phone call and went runnin' out the door." He went on, trying to make sense of it all. "She got into a black car I ain't never seen. I couldn't see who it was because the windows were so dark. She never said…" he trailed off, unable to continue.

Ace parked outside of Keisha's mother's house. The cops were leaving as they approached the door. Once inside, Keisha's mother totally broke down when she saw them. *"My Baby! Why, my baby! Who did this to my baby? She's gone Ace, she's gone!"* Rick held her as the reality of Keisha's death set in.

"Why?" screamed Jasmine, the only sister she had ever known was now gone. Rick's tears flowed freely. He was no longer able to hold them back. Ace sat emotionless thinking of how this could have happened. *Who? What? When? Where did I go wrong?* he asked himself.

The crying subsided long enough for Ace and Rick to pull themselves together to leave. Jasmine stayed with Keisha's mom.

"Don't worry," Rick consoled her. "The funeral is on us. We'll take care of everything."

As they were getting in the car, UC's Hummer pulled up. He and Amir got out. None of them uttered a word to one another, they just gave each other cold stares. If it were another time and place, shots would have been fired. UC and Amir walked in and Ms. Porter embraced them both. She gave them all the details that she knew and UC gave her a wad of money.

"This is for you and the children. If you ever need anything else just call me. I really had love for your daughter Ms. Porter,she was my baby," UC comforted.

Amir tried his best to soothe Jasmine who just kept saying how she and Keisha had been road dogs since elementary school.

"It's okay," said Ms. Porter embracing Jasmine, "I need you to be strong for me, Jazzy."

***

Ace and Rick went to tell Mrs. Prince the news. "Come back and get me later, Rick," he said, once they were inside. He called for his mom.

"Mom, come down here please." She came downstairs to

109

see what he wanted.

"What's wrong with you lookin' all sad?" asked Mrs. Prince.

"Mom, Keisha is dead," Ace quietly blurted.

It took Mrs. Prince a moment before she realized she had heard him correctly. "Dead. Where are the children? Who will keep them? They are supposed to be yours," she reminded him.

"Mom, we never found out if they were mine."

"Well, wouldn't you say that now is a good time?" she asked disgusted. "Ain't no sense in someone else raising your children boy," she scolded.

Ace looked at his mother with stress in his face. He couldn't believe she was going there right now.

"So you need to file for a blood test, ASAP!" said Mrs. Prince not letting up. "Let me call your sister." Mrs. Prince got on the phone and called her daughter, Tacurra. "You know that girl Keisha, your brother was dealing with for years? She got killed," she informed.

"Well, Mom, she was into a lot of sheisty stuff," said Tacurra, without sympathy.

"That's no way to be Tee-Tee, Ace might be the father of those children," she argued.

"What? My brother is nasty and she was a hood rat. If those kids are his, how come he never brought them around us?" Tacurra asked.

"You know he wouldn't bring those kids around Samira," Mrs. Prince reasoned. Tacurra thought a moment about what she was saying,

"Well, I gotta' go, Mom. I'll be there later to see about Ali."

Ace just stretched across his bed and reminisced on Keisha. When they first met, she was the baddest chick from the projects. *Thin, cute face, and a fat ass. Damn,* Ace thought with a

110

single tear running down his face. *What about the kids,* he thought. The little boy does have my eyes and Aceisha has my curls. *What will I tell 'Mir,* he pondered, *and what about Nikki, she's pregnant....* He could no longer think. Thankfully, the phone rang non-stop from everyone trying to get the scoop.

After answering a few calls, Ace turned the phone off, tired of the hood media and their versions of what happened. Frustrated by the event that hurt his heart, he had to admit to himself that he did have a special kind of love for Keisha.

Hours gone by, Ace awoke to the sound of voices downstairs. "Damn, I didn't even know I fell asleep", he said to himself aloud. He was curious about the voices belonged to. He looked downstairs and saw his sisters, Tacurra and Teresa and suprisingly, Samira. As they discussed Keisha, Ace crept downstairs to hear more clearly.

"She had two children," said Samira..

"Damn," was all Teresa could say shaking her head. "She got a bum rap. I feel sorry for her children," added Tacurra.

"Yeah well, we need to know if those children belong to Ace. We can't let anybody else raise them if they're his. That boy is crazy," Mrs. Prince said totally disgusted by the whole situation.

Samira spotted Ace on the stairs and simply rolled her eyes. The pain in her heart showed all over her face. Following Samira's gaze, Teresa looked up and saw her brother.

"Ali, are you alright?"

"Yeah, I'm fine," he said. "As Salaam Alaikum, 'Mir."

"Wa Lakum Salaam, Ali," she said shortly. "So when are you going to tell little Ali he has a brother and sister?"

"Look, all of y'all stay out my business. Who said those kids are mine?" Ace expressed somberly.

"First of all, who the hell are you talkin' to? Second of all, we're going to her house to talk to her people and see what's what," insisted Mrs. Prince.

"Yeah boy," chimed in Teresa, "you really need to handle your business."

Ace turned and headed back upstairs, totally unarmed for this losing battle. A few minutes later, there was a knock at the door.

"Babe, you okay?" asked Teresa peeking her head through his bedroom door.

"Yeah," he replied hesitantly. She gave her baby brother a hug. "I know we don't always get along, but I truly feel for that girl, and if those children are yours, they need to know not only little Ali, but us too. No child deserves to be without a father, especially if the mother isn't around. So, I'm here like always, but don't get cute thinkin' I'm gonna be babysittin' all the time," she kidded. "Thanks sis, that's why I love you," he said, kissing his sister on her forehead, honestly comforted for the moment.

***

Rick and Jasmine went to Keisha's to get some things for the kids and to check that the apartment was free of drugs. She cried the whole way there and it got worse when they pulled up and saw all the flowers, balloons, bottles of Moet, and blunts covering the sidewalk in memory of Keisha's life.

"Y'all niggas need to find out who killed my girl! That's fucked up, y'all did this shit," she spoke to no one in particular. Rick held Jasmine as the tears rolled down both their faces while they completed their tasks.

There was a knock at the door. "Hello, anyone here?" Nijah and Odaysha called upstairs. "We're upstairs gettin' some things for the kids," Jasmine could barely reply.

"We were wondering if you needed any help with the cooking or the cleaning for the funeral," the ladies tenderly offered, knowing how close Jazzy and Keish were.

Rick came down with bags of clothes for the kids. "Yo-I'ma be in the car waitin'. Take your time," he said, having to get out of there. In the car, he tried to put the pieces together about that day, but couldn't come up with anything.

Jasmine locked up the apartment. She gestured for Nijah and Odaysha to follow them as they headed to Keisha's mom's house. Rick dropped Jasmine off, feeling that at least she had her girls to console her for now. "Call me if you need anything," he said sadly, before pulling off. He turned on the radio and as bad as he already felt, Mariah and Boys to Men didn't help, "...*I know you're shining down on me from heaven/like the friends we've lost along the way...*"

Gratefully, Ace chirped him, sparing him the waterfall that begin to flow down his face. He wanted Rick to come get him from his mom's. "Alright, I'll be there in a minute. One."

With Rick on the way, Ace got himself ready to hit the block hard that night, not knowing what else to do. He made a quick call to Stacey before leaving the house. "Stacey, what up babe? One *of* of my peoples died, so I won't be up there tonight. I'll call you later. This is Ace." He was happy she didn't answer. Before being asked any more questions, Ace got out of the house to wait on the steps for Rick.

"Yo Ace, it's Kedar. Scrub-a-Dub is havin' somethin' for Keisha tonight. Pick a nigga up from the block," he chirped.

"Alright, I'm waitin' for Rick to come by, then we'll be through. Yo, what's the word on the street?"

"Man, ain't no word. Nobody's sayin' shit."

"Alright, man," said Ace, "One."

Mrs. Prince came outside just as he hung up with Kedar. "Ali, I need that girl's address and number so I can talk to her parents," she warned.

"Alright, Mom, I'll give it to you later," he said, "Damn," he mumbled. As hard as Mrs. Prince slammed the door when she went back in the house, that was a good indication that she was not playing. *What the hell is takin' Rick so long*? he thought anxious to roll. As soon as Rick turned the corner seconds later, Ace hopped off the steps and into the car.

"Man, my mom and them are buggin' out about the kids. I got to get a blood test or I will never hear the end of this shit. They even got Samira in there, in on it."

"Get outta' here nigga, a blood test after all these years; Richard is eight and Aceisha is two. You gotta' do what you gotta' do, I guess," said Rick.

"I know, right? My family is buggin' though," said Ace. Rick continued arguing his point, "Nigga you know they're yours. That girl been lovin' you since day one and no blood test can tell anybody that. Plus, why do that to them children? All they know is you as their dad."

"I wanna' be sure. I gotta' know. I mean, I'll look out for them on the strength but I need to be sure."

Kedar was where he promised he would be, on the block. Ace and Rick got out the car to get some love. Everybody expressed their condolences with pounds, sympathetic words, hugs and kisses. Ace normally loved to shine but it was church on the block, and it was more than he could stand. Keisha was a big part of the money making process. Now Ace realized, he would have to step up his game and that realization was a bit much.

Money was slow on the block; niggas were just around. "Let's get the fuck outta' here Rick," said Ace overwhelmed. "This block shit is too much for me." They went to Rick's and chilled
until nightfall.

Nikki was shocked as hell that not only did Ace answer his phone, but on the first ring too. "You coming over tonight?" asked Nikki, who was staying with Simone temporarily.

"Naa," said Ace. "It's something I need to talk to you about."

***

Keisha's funeral was held at Wright's Mortuary, the local funeral home that usually prepared all the young children to go home. It seemed they did a good job on those who were killed. The viewing was held from four to six, and cars were lined up outside the place as if it were a concert. Keisha knew loads of people through her affiliation with Ace. It was like a party at Club 2000. Even those who were struggling to eat, had on their best. Each of the different sets from around the city all arrived in limos, as if they were the immediate family.

Jasmine, Nijah and Odaysha walked in together; all checking on the children and Mrs. Porter before taking their seats. UC, Amir, Khaliq and Dominique who were recovering from a concussion, walked in together. UC provided Keisha's outfit and he went all out. Her dress was tailor made and her shoes were imported from Italy, custom-designed for her. Even under the circumstances, UC and Ace competed with each other. The flowers were so overwhelming from the two of them that Mr. Porter had to put some of them outside. Just to be smart, UC carried an arrangement, with their picture on the front from their trip to Vegas. And the whole city saw it because the whole city was there; North-side, East-side, West-side, South-side. No side was left out from saying their good-bye's.

Ready to move on with things, Mr. Porter had to remove Moet and Hennessey bottles, bags of weed, and hood flicks from his daughter's casket, before the services could even begin. Everybody wondered if heaven had a ghetto, right along with Tupac, who was playing in the sanctuary.

As the ushers escorted Keisha's children and her mother

to their seats, Mrs. Porter could barely stand. Ace sat up front, to be close by to comfort her. The family decided it was time to close the casket and the preacher rose to speak.

Everyone listened in silence, stirring only when Shahida stood to do her poem she had dedicated to Keisha and her life. It was called C.O.W. and all eyes focused on her, because when Shahida spoke, they knew it would be powerful.

"The death of Keisha should be a lesson for some and a warning for most, but I'm not here to preach; this is my poem, entitled Casualties of War:

## *C-O-W...*
*Fast cars, fast money and good times*
*All have a price*
*Whether you pay now or later,*
*Shit ain't fair in this life*
*Drinking, smoking weed*
*Stealing and getting hair weaves,*
*All desires-*
*None of the things I need*

*Taking life for granted,*
*Living like tomorrow's my advantage*
*No one knows my pain*
*Just that Keisha was my name*
*In this game,*
*Someone is always keeping score*
*And you need to know, in this life,*

*There will be casualties of war*
*And I, one of them.*"

Although no one wanted to hear the truth, Shahida's message was felt by all. Ace turned and looked at everyone with their tear-filled eyes, wanting to change. But knowing that they would all be smoking and drinking, in Keisha's honor, once they all left.

"OH GOD!!! WHY MY BABY?!! WHY?" Keisha's mom screamed. The ushers escorted her outside as everyone stood shoulder to shoulder and hot as a motherfucker, to view Keisha's body for the last time.

Jasmine and crew approached the casket with radio in hand, playing Keisha's favorite song, 'Bout My Paper, by Foxy Brown, "...*Who could talk about that paper better than me?/Who could stay hood so femininely?/Who stay on Fifth Avenue, spending them G's?/Who's just as controversial as Eminem be?...*" The emotion of it all overtook Jasmine, who started hollering and screaming and falling on the floor. Rick and Ace rushed to her aid and picked her up as she kicked and screamed, "Why? Why Keisha? We promised one would never go anywhere without the other?"

Jasmine's performance made even the children cry harder. With the mourning in full swing, people just started rushing the casket, whooping and crying and carrying on.

Rick peeped UC observing everyone, but showing no emotion himself. It took a few hours to completely clear the funeral home. Everyone left, blazing their blunts. "This is for you, Keish," as he poured out liquor on the sidewalk. "Hope there's a heaven for a G." It was the saddest funeral anyone had been to thus far.

The repast was held at Club 2000 where everyone gathered to eat and mingle. Still showing off, Little UC brought a dozen boxes of Crysta'l.

"Nothing but the best for my baby," he declared.

Ace simply looked at Rick as if to say, "You see this nigga?"

UC walked over to the bar, directly to where Ace and Rick sat, with hand extended. "No hard feelings man. I loved her just as much as you."

Ace half-way smiled and turned his head the other way.

"Fuck you then, you broke-ass nigga. I was tryin' to be nice," UC spat.

Ace rose from the barstool. Rick, not usually the peacemaker, held Ace back. "Chill man, this is her funeral."

Amir gritted on Rick something fierce and their eyes locked. If it weren't for Nadirah coming to talk to Rick, it would have been a rumble.

"Babe, I'm ready, so let's go," she said.

"Hey Ni-Ni," Amir teased. She rolled her eyes, hating for anyone to call her that. Just as Rick was about to jump, over walked Ms. Porter, with her ghetto self, "You disrespectful ass niggas! What y'all need to do is take your kids and bounce.

Rick, you take Richard and Ace take Aceisha," she instructed. Nadirah included her two cents,

"Yeah, Ace does need to take his kids."

"Oh no bitch. Stop actin' dumb.

Ace you take your daughter and Rick take your son," said Ms. Porter. Everyone looked puzzled and confused.

"Congratulations!" she announced. "You both got kids by her, that's what friends share!" Then she walked away.

"Nothing but the best for my Keisha," UC chuckled as he sat a bottle of Crysta'l on the bar between Ace and Rick.

Rick walked away angry and embarrassed with Nadirah basing on him.

"I know you didn't fuck that stink ho'! She used to be at our house, you dirty bastard…!"

Ace simply stood where he was, still mystified by what he had just heard. He left the club a few moments later, totally distressed. *What the fuck,* Ace thought confused, my boy was sleepin' with my ride or die chick all this time?

"What part of the game is that?" he called to ask Rick, not wanting to believe it. "My best friend-my brother?"

~*chirp*~"Whatever nigga," said Rick with Nadirah still ranking him in the background-Click.

***

Samira's phone rang and it was that Jersey number, again. *They won't leave you alone,* Samira thought, as she snatched the phone from the charger.

"As Salaam Alaikum," she greeted with annoyance in her voice.

"Hi, this is Stacey. I'm Ace's girlfriend and I saw your number on his phone list several times. May I ask who the hell you are?"

"First of all," said Samira steamed, "I don't appreciate you calling my house. Second, your dumb ass probably don't even know Ace's real name. Third, you'll never be his girlfriend. You're just some bitch he's using. And last, you will continue to see my number on his call list, you dumb bitch, so you better not call my house again!" Samira slammed down the phone, not liking the fact that she just acted completely out of character. She was out-done with Ace and all his bullshit; this call put the icing on the cake. Fuck the icing, she fumed, and all those bitches can have their cake!

A few hours later, Ace walked through the door, "Babe, I'm home." Samira had gathered all his things and had them waiting for him by the door. Ace looked down to see all his stuff in bags, then he looked up to see her coming downstairs with her game face on. From her expression, he didn't question whether or not she was playing; this time was definitely different. She started right in on him, "Look Ace now is not the time for you and me. I have dealt with your shit for way too long. All those different women, the lies, chicks getting killed, babies and bitches calling my crib. NO," she said pushing him away, "Enough is enough. If you love me like you claim you do then leave. My focus is on God; but at the end of the day, your focus is the streets, which will leave your ass all alone."

The pain shot right to his heart; he knew she was serious this time. He cried and pleaded with her, but she stared at him completely unmoved and emotionless. "This time is the last time-it's over," she said drained.

Ace gathered his things and left, hoping she would call him back. Instead, she slammed the door behind him.

"Damn, what am I gonna' have left?" he sobbed in the car. "My best friend was fuckin' my side bitch and now the love of my life is actin' stupid." Ace sat in the driveway just staring at the door and calling Samira on his cell. The phone just rang and rang, while she watched him looking pitiful from the window; she couldn't keep the tears from pouring forth if she tried.

# CHAPTER 8

## A Hustler

Awakening from a restless sleep after a long night at Stacey's, Ace could not stop thinking of Keisha and her murder. He had been spending more and more time with Stacey, out of the city and away from all the hype.  It was what he needed. Pancakes, turkey bacon and eggs scented the air, helping him to face the day.

Clearing his throat and wiping the sleep from his eyes, he reached down to feel around for his phone.  He checked to see who the four missed calls were from. They were all from Nikki. *Damn this chick really be buggin',* he thought the exact moment Stacey walked into the bedroom with a tray of breakfast for him. Ace put down his phone, smiled and sat up.

"Can't you leave that phone alone for just a few days?" she snapped.

"I got a lot of business that needs my attention; so no, I can't leave the phone alone," he explained. Anyway, you wanted them expensive meals, trips and shoes so am I supposed to ignore what you want?"

Unmoved by his explanation, Stacey sat the tray on his lap, sucked her teeth and turned to leave the room.  He just smiled and admired her ass bouncing as she stomped out with an attitude.

"Be easy," he called after her. "Me being here should be enough.  I'm here almost every night. What more do you want?" *Women are never satisfied,* he thought as he began to chomp down on his food. He was so hungry, he barely chewed.

His mind raced as he ate. He needed a quick scheme to get

money. Little did anyone know, but Keisha was the strength and brains of the empire. She knew who had it, how to cop it without gettin' caught and how to get rid of it in the middle of a drought.

After eating, he got up and went to the bathroom to shower, still trying to figure out the cash flow. As he eased into the wet soothing warmth, his mind ran all over the place. *I never realized how much of an asset baby girl was. Since Little UC was with Jasmine all night he couldn't have killed her, so who did? Was it the niggas we set up in Maryland or the ones we set up down Dover? It's been so many, I don't know who the fuck did it. Who the hell was in the car with the PA tags that Rick seen her leave in? Why the hell isn't anybody talkin'? Either they don't care or they don't have a clue...*

Ace became more confused the more he tried to make sense of it all. *How the hell can little Richard be Rick's son? My mans was fuckin' my shorty; I guess that's the game though..*

The warm water from the shower rolled down his face, washing away his tears. *And what the hell is Samira thinkin'. She never even responded to knowin' about the other kids? I haven't talked to Rick in like two weeks and we been best friends since we were knee-high to ants. Are we gonna' let Keisha's death end our friendship just like that? I got mad feelings for Nikki but I really don't want to ruin her life. She's such a good girl and she really is in love with me. I don't know how to let her go 'cause I wouldn't know what to do if I seen her with another cat. Samira leavin' my side got me completely losin' my mind. She's my everything and all that any man would ever need. Lord knows I put her through a lot of stuff that I'm gonna get back sooner or later. I just hope that it's not sooner...at the same time I can't get let my feelings for Stacey get too involved. I got enough on my plate already but she's here in a clutch.*

The bathroom was moist with steam and it hung in the bathroom like dense fog, perfectly camouflaging his tears. He silently released some of the pain that had been building up inside him. Thugs do cry. It's just that nobody sees. He snapped out of it and washed up, hearing Stacey move around in the bedroom.

She was sitting on the edge of the bed when he walked into the room. She noticed the far away, sad look on his face.

"Babe, what's wrong?" she asked concerned. She went to him and began massaging his neck and shoulders.

He shrugged her off saying, "Nothin' I can't handle."

He dried off, with her staring at him as if she had never seen him naked. "Are you still feeling some kind of way behind your cousin getting killed?" she probed.

"Yeah, she was a close cousin," he said with a slight smirk. "The game I'm in seems to have no rules, at least no rules to be fucked with. Now shit is hot on the block because of her killin'. It's gonna' be hard as hell for me to get money and I got a seed to feed along with my cousin's children, so I'm kinda' stressin' over this shit, feel me?"

He couldn't just leave it at that, "These are things your rich ass would never understand."

"What?" Stacey asked not about to let that shit go, regardless of whether he was sad or not.

"You obviously don't know me or where I come from," she hissed. "I had to work hard as hell to get where I am today. Do you have any idea what it's like to be a sistah in white male corporate America? Nothing was given to me. The same 'ill shit that happens to everybody happens to me too. I just choose to make my situation better. So don't give me that poor little project boy speech like I didn't have to struggle nigga!"

"Sorry babe, I didn't mean it like that. I'm just stressin' over this shit," he repeated.

Still feeling a bit warm from his last comment, Stacey informed him, "You shouldn't let money control your emotions. How much money were you getting anyway? You should have invested."

"Shoulda', coulda', but I didn't. The pot is low right

about now and shit ain't gettin' any better, but yeah you right, I shoulda' invested," he agreed.

"Well maybe tonight we can go over your situation and put our minds together to come up with a solution," she offered. Ace's eyes got big, "A solution?"

"Yeah, I am an accountant," said Stacey.

"That's what's up," said Ace, perking up for the first time that morning. "Let me look in my pot and I'll get back with you later, but for now I have a few things to handle in the city. I'm gonna take your car."

She wrapped her arms around his neck and stuck her tongue down his throat before answering, "Of course, anything for my Aceeee-pooh. Just be back for dinner. We can go to McCormick and Schmidt, on Broad in Philly, to grab a bite later."

"You always wanna spend money, man. Why can't you cook or somethin'?" Ace complained.

"Because I got it to spend," she announced. "So I'm still going even if you don't."

"Alright babe," he said giving in.

He started getting dressed when his phone vibrated. Stacey eyed the phone with venom in her eyes. He paid her no mind, smirked and walked out the room to answer it. "What up peoples?" he tried sounding neutral careful not to give away the gender of the person on the other end of the line.

"Peoples?" asked the voice on the other end. "Ace stop playin'."

"What's up?" he asked again, as he left the house. He paused to admire the Mercedes SLK 350 before getting in.

"Where have you been? I told you I wanted to talk to you and you've been avoiding me. If you don't want to be with me anymore, let me know," she whined.

"Girl, stop buggin'. I'll be there in a few," he said. *Damn, here goes the stress; these fuckin' women in my life are really gettin' on my nerves. I'm about to go solo,* he thought as he let out a little chuckle. *Yeah right, I love the life too much to let it go right now, honestly.* He loaded the six-CD player and allowed the music to set the mood for the ride home. He turned it on blast, reached in the ashtray for his blunt then blazed, speeding on the highway to Wilmington.

***

"Girl you crazy-Ace ain't shit! Stop callin' his sorry ass. He keeps duckin' you. Now you need to duck him," Simone said to Nikki, fed up. "I keep tellin' you he ain't the only baller in the city. Terrence likes you like that, and at least you know he'll spend time and money," Simone schooled.

"Whatever girl, I love Ace, and you saw what happened the last time I was kickin' it with Terrence at the basketball game; it was a big mess," Nikki reasoned.

Simone just rolled her eyes way up into her head and said, "Yeah right girl, you gonna see he ain't the one." Nikki leaned back on the couch and did damage on the bowl of cereal she was eating. She thought that maybe Simone was right. Then she thought about the life growing inside her and how it made her want Ace that much more. She was having even stronger feelings for him now than she had before.

"Okay girl-maybe you're right. If Ace comes here for me, just tell him I left; I'ma go upstairs and lay down. I'm tired."

In need of a break herself, Simone fired up a Newport and turned on *Homicide: Criminal Intent.* Within moments of her settling in to watch her show, just as the story line was being set up, a horn honked outside. Simone peeked out the window and saw Ace getting out the car. She hollered upstairs for Nikki, just to be smart but there was no peep from her. With the cigarette still hanging from her lips, she went to the door.

"Yo where's Nikki?" Ace asked with his infamous smirk on his lips.

"She left with her mother. She'll be back," she covered for her friend.

"Oh yeah? So can I get a quickie since you're alone?" he had the audacity to ask.

Simone hesitated, thinking of Nikki upstairs, and slammed the door in his face.

"Dumb bitch," he mumbled and jumped back in the car.

Only driving up the block, he couldn't help showing off. He honked for Kedar to come outside way before he was in front of the house. Then he parked, drawing all kinds of looks from pushing the exclusive Mercedes that hadn't even hit the market for the general public yet. He wanted everyone to know that he was still a baller and that he still had it all.

He got out of the car and walked past Gorilla and Manny, who were sitting on someone's steps on the corner. The men all gave each other pounds.

"How you feelin', Ak?" asked Manny.

"I can't complain," said Ace. "The game don't stop, the plays just switch."

"I heard that player," said Manny, nodding his head to the beat coming from the squatter that was parked on tenth Street. The tone seemed normal on the block-kids running around, girls eyeing the ballers and the fiends asking for handouts. Ace rested his back against a brick wall to wait for Kedar and just meditated on the scene.

"Ace," a girl whispered sensuously as she walked by. Ace simply smirked in her direction and as always, he watched her butt as she threw it down the street. His phone vibrated as he enjoyed the girl's ass show and when he checked to see if he wanted to accept the call, it was as if he had seen the boogeyman, it was Rick.

"Yo," Ace answered concealing his surprise.

"What up nigga? I guess we need to talk, huh?" asked Rick.

"I guess," said Ace. "I'm on the block."

"Alright. I'll be there in a few minutes. I have to drop my son off to my moms," said Rick.

"One," Ace acknowledged.

Ace chirped Kedar to get him moving. "Yo, I'm outside, you need to come on. What's the hold-up nigga?"

"Here I come. I'm just gettin' out the shower," explained Kedar.

To pass the time, Ace checked out what was going on down the street. He saw Nikki get in her car and speed off to 10th street. He yelled for her, but she either didn't want to respond or she didn't hear him, so he quickly chirped her phone. He got no response.

"Fuck her then," Ace said. He experienced a tinge of shock at the possibility that Nikki was actually giving him shade.

As if things weren't hectic enough, Detective Shaffin rode by Ace slowly, just as Kedar was finally coming out of the house. The detective gritted Ace down and stopped his car directly in front of where he stood on the corner.

"Hey Ace-zee-toe," said the cop, "I see you huggin' the block. What- you lonely?"

Ace didn't feed into his taunts and just walked towards 10th Street. He remembered that this was the same cop who locked up his cousin Ken-Ken, for allegedly possessing two keys of coke and a gun with four bodies on it a few years back. The detective found witnesses when there were none and it seemed the entire justice system was in cahoots to give Ken-Ken life.

Shaffin drove off only when Ace was further away.

"That prick is always fuckin' with you man. What? He gay or somethin'? He got a hard on for you?" asked Kedar.

"Yeah, I hate that faggot ass cop. He's just waitin' to catch me up in some shit, Kedar," Ace said.

"Yo let's go down Simone's and play the game," suggested Kedar since they were walking in that direction anyway.

"I'm with that," said Ace. He called Simone as they got closer. *~chirp~* "Yo 'Mone."

"What, Ace, what?" She could not understand why she was having such a hard time watching her show undisturbed.

"Open the door. Me and Kedar are comin' to play the game," said Ace.

"Alright," she said, getting up to let them in. They were already on her step, when she opened the door. Rick was parking in front of her house as Ace and Kedar were going in. Simone noticed him first, turning her frown upside down. "Richarddddd!"

## The Lies Hustlers Never Tell

Trips from Miami to Aruba
Cali to Cancun
Cute nigga stay laced,
Money ain't a thing
When the hustler's in the room
Fur coats and diamonds
Women,
He wines & dines 'em
A definite baller
And got money for a lawyer
Got chicks who ride or die,
With his name tatted on their brain
Get low, even rob a nigga
Just to save his name
Get respect from any side
Other niggas he claims
Niggas know a true baller
So they respect the game.


A HUSTLER

One of the biggest pluses to being an accountant was the ability to work from home, and Stacey was definitely thankful for that, as she got out the list of numbers she had copied from Ace's phone.

Samira's was the first, and only number, she paid special attention to. That sistah was very direct and to the point, she observed. Stacey felt threatened. As she reflected on their brief conversation, the fact was that she'd heard something in Samira's voice that caused her to take her very seriously. She was uncompromising about what she'd told her about Ace. Entering anywho.com under the reverse phone look-up, she got Samira's address in Newcastle to keep on tuck. *Never know when I might have to show up at her door and check things out for myself*, she thought deviously.

Jolted by the piercing ring of the telephone, Stacey wondered *when the hell everybody in the office actually worked*. It seemed to her that they were always on the phone calling to bug the hell out of her.

"Yes," she snatched up the receiver, speaking in a tone of aggravation from being disturbed one too many times. "Hello Ms. Lockett, this is Kayla. I hate to disturb you but we were working on closing out the JB Mazlo books and we're missing the financial report of Mr. Mazlo's real estate holdings. Do you have them there with you?" Glancing around her desk, Stacey had the report in front of her. "Yes Kayla, I have it here with me. I'm reviewing it one last time. I'll send it by courier in about an hour or two."

"Okay," said Kayla, "I'll be looking out for it."

JB Mazlo was a self-taught, highly successful Interior Designer who owned several upscale bed-and-breakfasts' across the country. They were the personal playgrounds to some of the world's wealthiest people. He was also one of the most financially irresponsible people Stacey had the displeasure of keeping books for. But it was sort of a family obligation.

JB and her dad were fraternity brothers and life-long friends, so in exchange for keeping her home cutting-edge and state-of-the-art, she handled his finances. He had open accounts all over the world due to his love of fine things, and he also recently passed away leaving a bunch of open credit lines that she was responsible for handling.

She suddenly discovered a solution to all of Ace's money problems. *It'll take months before Mazlo's mess is totally straightened out*, she thought. *Nobody even knows about most of these accounts but in the meantime. ...*

She excitedly called Ace to tell him of her scam, but his voice mail picked up on the first ring. "This nigga swears he's so busy", she said to herself as she redialed. She ended up leaving a message. "Hey babe, I've got the answer to what we talked about earlier, so give me a call back as soon as you get this message." She hung up satisfied, knowing that by the time he called back there would be thousands of dollars waiting for him. All it took was for her to call and report the cards stolen, because she hadn't notified JB's creditors of his death. She would change the address on the accounts, get replacements for the old cards, set up new Pin numbers and Voila! What she needed from him was an address where the new cards could be sent. *As a matter of fact*, she thought wickedly, *I already have one.*

***

Stacey and Ace went on a roaring rampage of identity theft fraud using JB Mazlo's information. They bought ridiculous things and got plenty of cash, creating a trail leading right back to them in the process. What they didn't count on was that old seemingly care-free and irresponsible JB had been honest enough with himself about himself to protect himself and his loot, by hiring a world renowned risk management company that watch-guarded his assets and his back. The CEO of that company was not only a loyal and frequent VIP guest at his property on Martha's Vineyard, but also a close friend.

Turns out that, as they got away with more and more, they got sloppier and sloppier. They had unwisely sent so many credit cards to the same address, Samira's, it was not hard for the private investigators to piece the puzzle together. Plus, the fact that Stacey possessed much knowledge of his multi-million dollar network, put her in a position to be surveillanced.

Within two weeks, Detective Shaffin showed up at Stacey's house, three o'clock in the morning, to place both of them under arrest. They were both knocked out from having wild sex with their new sex toy, courtesy of JB.

# Chapter 9

## The Game Don't Change

"Mr. Prince, bag and baggage!" Ace hopped off his bunk leaving all his things there for his celly. "Yo man, I won't be seeing you here again," he said right jolly. "This little fifteen months made me a believer that jail ain't for me. This is not the place for a man to be a man. You can't eat, sleep, or shit without another man telling you what to do. I'm gonna do right by my baby moms and take care of my children. That's my plan." He stood by the bars waiting for them to open.

"Okay Mike-Mike, wit' ya stinkin' ass. I'm outta here," he said talking shit to the rough shaven, stocky, heavily tatted, white guard.

"You'll be back," Mike-Mike promised with a knowing smile. "They always do."

"Don't think so," Ace retorted as he slid out the jail cell guided by thoughts of Samira. He could not wait to get home and show her how deep his love for her ran. He wanted to honor her as his queen.

Getting closer to the door, he could see his sister, Tacurra with Aceisha by her side. "Hey Brother," she greeted her baby bro' with open arms and a warm kiss. "Look at you all cute and strong."

"Daddy, Daddy!" Aceisha ran from behind her Auntie and jumped into his arms, long silky pony-tails flying. Looking down in the face of his daughter, he saw Keisha and that hurt him to his heart. He fought to hold in his tears as he kissed and hugged his baby girl.

"Where's little Ali?" he asked Tacurra, putting Aceisha down. "We haven't seen him in months," she said somberly. "I've tried to get him, and so did Mommy, but Samira is never home and she changed the phone number. I don't know what's up with that shit. That girl been buggin' and she's not usually like that. I thought you did something else to her."

"Man, I haven't seen her or my son in a few months," Ace said concerned. "At first they were visiting me every week, but you know the babe Nikki?"

"Nikki who?" asked Tacurra unable to keep track of them all.

"You know the babe with the Lex'. Well she got a baby by me," he confessed. Tacurra's eyes got big and she could not believe what she had just heard.

"A baby? You are so sneaky and dumb. These chicks come with a big butt and you just lose your damn mind!"

"Listen man, they both came to visit at the same time a few months ago." That really got her attention. "You lyin'," she said soaking up the juice. "I haven't seen Samira since," he said sadly.

They exited the prison and Ace paused a moment to turn his face up to the sun, once again, a free man. Tacurra, however, was still stuck on the baby news. She looked at him shaking her head.

"Nikki, Nikki, now which one was she again?"

"She was the babe with the Lex' truck. The blue jawn I used to have," he further described.

"You sure didn't write home tellin' us about that one," she said, "Boy-you crazy! You knew you had little Ali and Aceisha! Why are you takin' it upon yourself to populate the city of Wilmington? And to top it off, you haven't even told Mommy about it yet. She's gonna' snap!"

"Man look. I ain't tryin' to hear all that! Give me time to

134

breathe, damn, I just maxed out!" He glanced around the prison grounds, bidding farewell and trying desperately to block out his sister's nagging which sounded like, '*wog, wog, wog...*' in his ears.

His thoughts raced down the highway as fast as Tacurra was driving the car. He couldn't wait to take a hot shower, at home, and to hold Ali and Samira in his arms. "Yo Tee-Tee!" he had no choice but to yell over her, "Let me see your cell phone a minute!"

She handed it over mindlessly, still ranting, " Why the hell didn't you strap that thing up, boy ?"

He called Samira's house just to get the mechanical lady saying that the number he had reached had been disconnected. Then he tried her cell phone, thinking that she'd never change that number. There was a busy signal indicating that the number was in fact, disconnected. Ace sat puzzled and Tacurra stared at him with disgust, finally giving her jaws a rest.

"Who you call?" she asked.

"Man- none of 'Mir's numbers work. What's up with that?"

"I told you she's missing in action; M-I-A," Tacurra spelled out, "You shoulda' been kept it real with her. If I was her, I woulda' been got rid of your ass anyway, love or not."

"Well maybe she's just on some 'in the box' mode. After I get fresh, I'ma go pass and scoop up her and Ali and do the family thing. This time things will be better." His intentions were true.

"Yeah whatever; you always say that shit. Why should she believe you now?" said Tee-Tee keeping it real with him.

Ace wondered why there wasn't a slew of niggas waiting for him at the crib as they pulled up. He entered his mother's home to find her sitting patiently waiting for her baby. "Hey baby," she kissed and hugged him like no one else in the world but his mom could, "How I missed you. I hope and pray that was your last time in there. You really had me worried. It wasn't pleasant at all having you in that place."

"I know Mom, you won't have to worry about me going back there. That place ain't fit for a king!" he smiled, thankful to see his mom's face again. The tender moment was cut way short when Tee-Tee came in the house, lips flapping a mile per second, "Mom! Ali got some news for you. You might have another grandbaby!"

Having had enough of her and her big mouth, Ace slapped her in the forehead with an open palm, causing her neck to snap back as if were on a rubber band. Tee-Tee drew back her fist, but she had to say something first before she struck, "Look nigga, I ain't none of them girls you date. I will fuck you up!"

Mrs. Prince thankfully stepped in, "Y'all stop that! Ali what is she talking about?"

He just looked at her, somewhat relieved that at least now she knew. He hated lying to his mom. From the look on his face, Mrs. Prince knew the truth, "I ain't for all this mess, Ali! You need to wrap up before you have five and six kids running around, all with different mothers!"

"Alright already," he said racing upstairs to avoid her wrath. Once in his room he took it all in, happy to be home, then he stripped. It was definitely time for the much anticipated shower.

Sitting on his bed, he looked in the closet for something to wear, still dripping with a towel around his waist. This was the first time in a long time that he didn't have anything new hanging in his closet. *I've only been gone fifteen months, the game couldn't of changed that much*, he thought, so he slipped on some Dickies and Tims'. He then grabbed the cordless and made some calls. Kedar was first on the list, "Kedar, what's the deal playboy? It's Ace-zee-toe."

"Hey Ak," said Kedar, happy to hear from his street partner. "I just maxed out, come scoop me up," said Ace glad that somebody seemed happy to hear from him.

"Alright, I'll be there in a few, let me finish playin' *Madden*," said Kedar faithfully.

He lay back on his bed and dialed the next number, "Hello, can I speak to Nikki?"

"She's not here. May I ask whose calling?"

"Yes ma'am, this is Ace," he responded politely. "Is the baby there?"

"No. Nikki and the baby don't live here but I'll be sure to tell her that you called."

He hung up wondering if everybody was incognito these days. He next tried Samira's number again, in case he had dialed the wrong number the first time, only to get the same result he got the first time. Calling her people's house looking for her was out of the question. The lecture he was sure to get was more than he could handle.

He thought and thought until he remembered, "Damn that's right-Simone!" he said out loud. "Let me call her, I know I can hit that right quick." He had to laugh at himself before he finished dialing her number because he never thought that he would be calling her on his first day out. "Yo Simone," he said slightly disguising his voice.

"Who this?" she asked not recognizing who it was on the other end.

"It's Ace. It hasn't been that long since you heard my sexy ass voice," he said confidently.

"Oh, what up?" she responded nonchalantly.

"Yo, I'm about to come through and hit that for old times sake."

Simone chuckled. "Kedar said he'd be there in a minute. He just left to scoop you up."

"Kedar?" he asked as if he didn't hear her correctly. "What-you fuckin' Kedar now?"

"Nigga you was never my man, so what difference do it make to you if I'm fuckin' Kedar or not?" she snapped.

"That's gansta'! Where your girl Nikki at?" he asked.

"You know we ain't friends no more but you can probably find her on the West-side with her man and baby," said Simone all too happy to bait him.

"Who her man?" he asked.

"You know she fucks with Terrence and come to find out she been fuckin' with him for a minute," she said reeling him in.

"Oh, that's what's up! This is the same nigga I had beef with 'cause of her, so how the fuck can she have my baby around that hatin' ass cat?"

Satisfied with herself, Simone cut it short. "Well enough with the interrogation nigga. Kedar is on his way." She slammed the phone in his ear to signify the end of their conversation.

"Bitches ain't shit!" he said as the phone erupted in his ear with a bang.

He reflected on things for a while when his mom called for him, "Ali, Kedar is down here."

He got up and headed downstairs to see his boy. "I see you got your weight up nigga," said Kedar as they gave each other a hug.

Mrs. Prince, although touched by the scene, warned her son, "Ali, don't go back on that block."

"Mom, I'm only going to scoop up little Ali," he said, genuinely wanting her to be easy as they walked out the door.

Ace felt a bit warm and fuzzy at the sight of Kedar's squatter. He had run the streets all the time in that car. They got in and Ace settled into the passenger seat. "Yo, you wanna' spark somethin'?" asked Kedar.

"Naa," said Ace, "I'ma chill for right now. If I can go fifteen months without a smoke, I can go a little bit longer."

"I heard that," said Kedar as he drove off the block.

"So you fuckin' the babe, huh?" asked Ace.

Kedar lit up, "Yeah nigga! And she a freak too, *wog, wog, wog...*" Without even realizing he had done it, he filtered out the bullshit as Kedar talked. When Kedar took a breath, Ace said, "Yo, ride through the Westside."

"I thought we were goin' to Newcastle," Kedar questioned the sudden change in route.

"I need to see that nigga, Terrence," Ace said eyes telling the whole story.

"Man look, I'm all highed up and I don't feel like that beef shit. Next thing you know, I'll get shot again," Kedar complained.

"You still actin' like a pussy man? Then let me hold your car for a few hours, you punk ass nigga. You act as if I'ma let some shit happen to your ass." He was annoyed by Kedar's caution.

Kedar pulled up in front of Simone's and gladly got out so Ace could handle his own shit. As he was getting out the car from his side to get in the driver's seat, he heard, "Aaaaaace!" It was Simone standing in the doorway, staring at him as if she could eat him alive. He just looked at her and thought, *Yeah right!* as he directed the car towards the West-side.

It was packed as usual, on the Westside. Ace rode through slowly digging the scene he had not seen in a minute. He parked by West Center City where everybody played ball and got out of the car. He shook a few hands all the while scoping out the area for any signs of Terrence. Standing on the corner of 6th and Madison, he watched the young boys play ball.

Out of the corner of his eye, he saw a gray Acura MDX drive up and park. This cat, Artega hopped out of the driver's side and gave Ace a smirk. The passenger door then swung open and Terrence got out holding a male toddler; he didn't even notice Ace on the other side of the street. Ace's face dropped, he didn't know whether to say anything or not. *My son,* he thought, *this nigga is sportin' my son. Man, that bitch Nikki know I will fuck both of them up.* He watched, as if in a trance, Terrence's every step as he and the child walked into the Center.

"Ace baby, what up?" broke his daze. He turned to see Jasmine, in Little UC's Hummer parking. She got out and gave Ace a big hug.

"What's up, baby boy? When you get out? Lookin' good as usual," she said sizing him up, "I see why Keisha loved you so much, you fine as shit! But what you doin' over here, the game is inside the Center?"

"I'm just rappin' to a few cats, gettin' caught up," he replied happy to be this connected to Keisha.

"Yeah? You better stay outta' trouble. I pick your daughter up every other weekend. She looks just like Keisha," said Jazzy.

"Word? Good lookin'. You were Keisha's truest friend," said Ace sincerely. She smiled and turned to continue on her mission.

"Well you take care of yourself and stay outta' trouble," she reiterated as she stepped back into the Hummer, music on blast as she drove off.

Ace's thoughts returned to Terrence. *I'm not even gonna snap. I just got out, so I'll let that nigga breathe for now, but I sure am gonna slap that bitch once I see her.* With that infamous smirk on his lips, he got back in the squatter and pressed on his journey to Newcastle.

*I've only been gone fifteen months,* he thought, *and life sure didn't stop for me.* He comforted himself on the ride with visions of Samira and his son, and the plans he had for them as a family. He knew if anybody would be by his side right now, it would be Samira. They made a pact for life that she would always be his. He also knew he had done her dirty but she had God and she had to forgive. He couldn't wait to see her.

A look of confusion crossed his face as he parked on the

street. The car that was in her driveway prevented him from whipping in there as he always did. He hesitated getting out of the car, and stared at the vehicle in the driveway wondering to whom it could possibly belong. *Whoever it is, sure is ballin'*, he thought as he eyed the custom Volvo S80.

He rang the doorbell twice and patiently waited for Samira to answer the door. He was so hyped on seeing his family, he tried to peek in the window but the curtains were doing their job in blocking the view in. Just then, the door opened, "As Salaam Alaikum," a tall brother with a medium build greeted.

"Wa Lakum Salaam," said Ace obviously surprised. "I think I have the wrong house," he said turning to leave.

"Who you looking for, Brother?" the guy asked.

"Samira," replied Ace.

The dude smiled and said, "This is the right house, Brother. Come in." As he opened the door a little wider and stepped back, Ace walked in and simply stood there. "Brother, please remove your shoes and wait here. I'll go get Samira. By the way, my name is Abdul Kareem and you are?" he asked.

"Ace, nigga you know who I am."

Let's not be stupid," Ace said with indignation. Ignoring the snide remark, Abdul started to go get Samira, but she was already on her way out of the kitchen wearing nothing but a long silk nightgown. She stopped dead in her tracks when she saw Ace standing there. She knew this day would come.

Forgetting how happy he was supposed to be, Ace asked, "Samira, who that nigga?" With that, Brother Abdul Kareem went upstairs to get Ali.

She looked Ace directly in his eyes, without blinking and said, "That is my husband. You are more than welcomed to be a part of your son's life, but you must call before you come over and make arrangements to visit first. Don't just show up and please have a little respect."

"What? Man, I ain't tryin' to hear that shit," said Ace feeling too stunned to yell.

Samira was about to say something else, but cut it short as Kareem followed little Ali downstairs. "Daddy, Daddy!" screamed Ali, as he ran to his father and jumped on him, hugging and kissing. "I missed you!" Samira and Kareem looked on as Ali reconnected with his dad. Samira turned and began up the stairs.

Ace put Ali down and looked up at Samira. "Yo 'Mir. 'Mir, I need to talk to you. Come back down here before I snap." She didn't respond nor did she turn around. She simply kept climbing.

"So that's how it is?" Ace's heart shattered. "You got married to a nigga. I only did fifteen months!" he screeched.

Brother Kareem allowed Ace time to let the news sink in before saying, "Listen Brother, this is my home and my family. I ask that you respect that."

"Fuck you nigga! I ain't tryin' to hear all that shit! 'Mir!" he screamed. At this point, little Ali was scared motionless because he had seen his dad in action before when he got angry. Ace was oblivious to everything except Samira.

"You don't even love this nigga. You don't even know him! Who the hell is he?" his voice cracked.

"Let me talk to you for a second, Brother, before things get out of hand, which neither you nor I need."

Abdul Kareem leaned over and whispered to Ali to go upstairs with his mom while he talked to his father. He squared up with Ace and said, "Listen man, I don't know you, and don't care to. I do know that I love your son as if he were mine and I love his mother the same and she is mine. I don't know what you did or didn't do, but the bottom line is that not only as a Muslim man, but as a man, in general, I'm doing what I'm supposed to do for my family."

"You can't just come in here and play thug, Brother, so let's get clear on some things, don't let this thob fool you. The Muslim wear can come off. The only reason that we ain't at blows right now is because of my love for my family. I want you to give me the respect that I've given you."

Ace's face was as red as a ripe apple. "Alright Ak, I got you. Just send my motherfuckin' son back downstairs 'cause he's goin' with me."

"Okay Brother," said Kareem. "No need to be so hostile. Salaam Alaikum, Brother."

"Yeah," said Ace still tough. "Wa Lakum Salaam."

He could barely hold himself together as he waited for Ali. His emotions raged. If anyone was to be by his side, it was Samira. She was there through the late nights, the cheating, the babies. *I know I fucked a lot of babes, but my heart always stayed with her...how the fuck could she do this to me, get married...I thought. I had time if I didn't have anything else...she said she'd always be here...I thought I had time....*he thought. His heart was on the floor along with the solitary tear drop that refused to stay in his eye. Thankfully, Ali came downstairs. "Daddy, what's wrong?" he asked sensing a change in his father.

"Nothing man," said Ace holding his son's hand tenderly as they walked out the door. "Daddy gonna take you to Dave and Buster's to play some games," he promised as he made sure Ali buckled up.

"I was just there yesterday with Brother Kareem," Ali innocently informed him. "He's cool Dad." Ace looked at his boy lovingly and said, "Is he? Well let's go see grandmom then. You haven't seen her in a while and she misses you."

Somehow they made it to their destination safely and Ace was grateful for it. He couldn't tell anybody how he got there if he tried. He opened the door and Ali practically knocked his mom-mom down with the force in which he hugged her.

Then he saw his sister, "Hey 'Isha," he greeted her. Aceisha ran to her big brother and hugged him giggling. After settling down the kids with a snack, Mrs. Prince turned to her son, noticing his puffy red eyes as soon as he had walked in.

"What's wrong with you Ace? Why is your face so swollen?"

"Nothing Mom," he quickly answered. "Ali wanted to see you. I'ma take Kedar his car. I'll be right back." He left the house with the swiftness, hoping to outrun the tears. He drove around the city for hours, repeatedly listening to Anthony Hamilton pine away for *Charlene*. Rick's voice whispered in his ears the whole time, *"Man, you need to chill and do right by Samira,"* and he couldn't shake it.

His overwhelming thirst gave him something else to focus on for the moment, so he stopped at Kennedy Fried Chicken to get a Mistic. After paying for his drink, he turned to leave and saw Nikki was standing there with her mouth wide open. She wasn't trying to see him.

"Yo, what up?" said Ace. "I can't get a hug or nothin'?" Although he did her dirty, she still loved him, so she embraced him. "Why haven't you brought the baby to see me?"

Finally able to speak, she said, "Umm, I didn't know you were home."

"Yeah, I heard you with Terrence now. I guess you just hopped on the next nigga's dick, huh?"

"Look Ace, I gotta get my food and get to class. I'll call you later to talk to you."

"That's what's up. You still in school? How am I gonna get in touch with you?"

"Call my house, I'll get the message."

"Call your house? I want to see my motherfuckin' child," he moved on her and grabbed her arm.

"Look Ace, don't make a scene and let me the fuck go," she said yanking her arm away from him.

Ace was taken aback, just a little, by her new aggression, but he didn't let her know. "Man, you gonna' make me snap! Don't be havin' that nigga around my son, either."

"Okay, okay," she said as she rushed out the door with her food, nearly forgetting her change. She decided as she screeched off that it was probably best to wait awhile before telling him that the reason he saw Terrence with the baby, was because he was actually Terrence's son, not his.

Ace stood stuck for a moment. It was like everybody forgot that he was just the baller of the year. He unglued himself from the spot where he stood and exited the place. A couple of neighborhood girls hollered at him as he got in the car. Ace smiled back and pulled off thinking how it seemed like the game had changed.

He continued to ride through the city reminiscing. The tears from earlier had dried up to anger now. *Yeah, I'ma get back on top again,* he determined, *and Nikki and Samira is gonna wanna get back with me.* He let out a chuckle in spite of himself, *who would have thought Samira would ever leave me. I thought I had time with her if I didn't have anything else.* The car behind him honked because the light had changed.

Back at his mom's, Ace looked forward to spending time with his children. He leaned back on the couch to watch them play with each other. Every time he looked at Aceisha, he saw Keisha.

He drifted back to another time long ago when he first saw Keisha in the hallway at school. Her gear wasn't the most tactful, but she had a big butt and a cute face.

"Keisha, when you gonna let me take you out?" he remembered asking her. She just giggled and said, "Never nigga, I don't do light-skinded," as she walked away switching and laughing. He followed her. "Just let me take you out one time and I bet you'll never do dark-skinned again, with your pretty self."

"Whatever Ace," she replied, "You got a girl, so stick to her all covered up," referring to Samira being a Muslim. "Yeah, I got a girl, but I'ma get you real soon," he said plotting on the booty.

After school that day, he pulled up in his pink low-rider, blasting Rob Base, "*...it takes two to make a thing go right/it takes two to make it outta' sight...*" "Keisha let me take you home. You don't have to walk," he tried to sound suave even yelling over the music.

"Yeah it is cold," she shivered, "I'll go only if Jasmine can come too."

"Sure," he said as he lifted the back seat for Jasmine. When she snuggled in and warmed up a bit, she looked around the car and said, "Nice. What your girl gonna say about this?" With the smirk that had become legendary in the streets, he said, "I don't know. What you gonna say about this Keish?" She blushed at his charm and had been in his life from then until the end of her life.

"Daddy, daddy," Aceisha broke his revelry, yanking on his pant leg. "Ali took my doll's head off." Keisha still on his brain, he abruptly disciplined Ali. "Yo boy, give her back her doll and put the head back on."

Mrs. Prince called everyone to dinner before things got really crazy. "Come on children, let's get ready to eat," she said setting the table. Everyone sat at the table to break bread as a family, including his sisters. This brought joy to Mrs. Prince to have them all together again.

Ace, on the other hand, felt incomplete without Samira by his side. He remembered many meals like this when they were younger.

146

"What's wrong, Ace?" asked Teresa, seeing something was bothering him. Before he was able to say anything, Tacurra chimed in, "Maybe it's the new baby."

"Stop being rude," snapped Mrs. Prince. "Ace, what's wrong?" No longer able to hide his torment, he confided in his mom.

"It's like I thought the world would stop and wait for me, but it didn't. I thought the streets was my main man, but they ain't. I thought I had time to waste and that Samira would always be there, but she ain't. And out of everything that I've been through, the main thing that's killing me, is losing her."

It pained Mrs. Prince to see her baby so deeply troubled but she listened anyway. "The game sure didn't stop for me!" he blurted as he hung his head. Then he looked at his children and said to them, "Jail is not the look, y'all, you hear me?"

Mrs. Prince excused them to give their father an adult moment. With no compassion, Tacurra snickered and said, "Yeah it sounds good but…" Mrs. Prince nudged her before she could finish her sentence. Ace just looked around the table and said, "Whatever." Then he stood up and went upstairs, with his kids happily following.

He gave the kids their baths and put them to bed. Then he kicked it on the phone with a few old friends before calling it night, welcoming the relief of sleep.

*Shahida T. Fennell*

Time, oh time waits on no one
The clock strikes and that minute is over
The game ain't changed, just the paint job
And now they cop Benzes instead of Ranges
The passenger got booted for the latest dame

I mean, niggas go to jail, but the doors revolve
A nigga comes out; showers, shoes buffed, fresh taper
Getting hit off by the latest players
And he done read far too many Donald Goines books
not to get paper
Now he chasing
Although the respect still remains
Some have forgotten his name
You know the young boys coming up
on the block getting change
They just like you when you were their age
Wild, uncontrollable, middle finger in the air
So who's to blame
Bitches done got hot,
Now they hop on the next nigga's knot
You a legend, no doubt
But some forgot
'Cause time waits on no one
What's your name?
The clock strikes but that minute is over.


## TIME WAITS ON NO ONE

148

The next morning, Ace was more than ready to be on a mission. His sister left the car she didn't use anymore, for him to ride around, an '88 Honda Accord. He was not used to driving around in a hooptie, but it would have to do for now.

His children were already up and dressed, courtesy of his mother. So after breakfast, he was out the door. His mom called him back in handing him the phone. It was Samira.

"Yo," he said coolly. "Ali, when are you bringing my son home?" she dug right into him.

"What? He's my son too, and I haven't seen him in almost two years, stop buggin'. I'll bring him when I bring him," and he banged on her. Hearing her voice cut his heart.

Determined to make a few rounds and touch base with some people, his kids were his side-kicks. He drove to The Lounge amazed at the renovations and additions that had taken place since he was last there. The upgrades included, pool tables, vending machines, flat screen televisions that hung on the walls and a game room.

"Playboy," he said walking up on Spice. "This is how a nigga been livin' since I been gone?" Spice grinned from ear-to-ear recognizing the voice right away.

"You know business, on the legal side, is where the motto is: If you stick and stay, you'll get your pay! It gets greater as it gets later baby!" he said hugging Ace.

Ace looked around at the place and saw how truly happy Spice was. "Damn, I guess that ain't just a sayin' huh?" Uncle Spice admired the little ones, "Damn, look at your children. They got big since I last saw them. This guy looks just like you when you were his age," he said shaking little All's hand. "And your daughter looks just like Keish. Damn, its crazy, her not being here and shit, just crazy."

"Man look, the game don't love anyone. I know that for sure. Did you hear that Samira got married?" asked Ace.

149

"Well you know, how long was she supposed to wait on you and your bullshit?" Spice said.

"You right. Cut me like a knife-first Keish, then jail, now 'Mir. What can go wrong next?"

"Yeah I hear you talkin'. You act like you done five years nigga, you only done fifteen months!" the older, wiser man said tickled.

"And for sure, I'm a believer! Jail ain't the look! One thing I do know, I respect talkin' to you Spice. You always keep it real and give it to me straight."

"They never did find out who killed Keish, huh?" asked Spice. Ace simply shook his head. "What you gonna do with your life now?" Spice asked, honestly interested in his answer.

Ace went blank, never thinking he would ever need to answer that question. He shrugged his shoulders and headed for the door.

"You know a nigga always run from real conversation," observed Spice. "Oh yeah, the boy Little UC is havin' a celebrity basketball game in honor of Haji and Shakir. You know them niggas made numbers seven and ten in the NBA draft?"

"Yeah," said Ace, grateful for the change in subject. "Haji sent me clips when I was in the joint. I'm proud of them both and I will be there for sure." The two men extended hands to give each other dap. "Stay outta trouble," said Spice, only half joking.

Ace decided that he wanted to spend the day with all his children, so he went to Nikki's house to see if he could get the baby. No answer. The East-side was his next stop. Simone was in the door as usual, so he parked. "What up chicken-head?" Her face beamed.

"Look at those children!" she said really delighted to see them. "They look just like you," she said.

"Yeah, I know," Ace said proudly. "Where Kedar?" Simone pulled on her cigarette and blew smoke rings for the kids before she answered.

"Up the block. Shit ain't changed. The block still bubbles."

Ace and the kids walked Clifford Brown Walk. He noticed all the new faces and a few old ones sprinkled in the mix as he approached and hollered outside for Kedar.

The front door opened and Kedar's sister, Aaliyah stood there smiling at him. Ace was genuinely surprised to see her. "Look how you grew up. I haven't seen you in years," he said. She smiled even wider and reached out to give him a hug.

"Damn, living down south with your pops got you real healthy," he admired her thick legs, slim waste, and just right butt.

At that exact moment, he envied the denim and he totally understood why Ginuwine would sing a song that talked about *'those jeans'*.

Kedar appeared, coming down the steps bringing a halt to the fantasy. "Yo, stop lookin' at my sister like that," he said, bass in his voice and watching Ace drool over Aaliyah.

The fellas reminisced on old times and played the X-Box half the night until Ace decided to drop off little Ali home to his mother.

Samira and Kareem were taking in the grocery bags when Ace pulled up. He shined the high beams on them and laughed. They shook their heads at his level of immaturity. Samira whispered something to her husband then walked over to the car. She kissed and hugged her baby and sent him in the house.

Satisfied little Ali was out of ear-shot, she looked at him and said, "Ace, we need to talk."

"Do we?" he smugly replied. "I'm listening," he said staring off into space, wanting to avoid the truth of her what she prepared to say. Words could never describe the pain he felt at that moment.

"It's funny how you can't handle the fact that I'm married," she began. "But I had to handle you dealing with Keisha, Nikki, Stacey and a few other heifers you banged along the way."

"It's also mighty funny how you have a few children on the side, since we were together over our ten year relationship, yet Ali is my only child. How many days did I have to sleep alone? Did it ever occur to you how I felt? I've watched you drive different women's cars, taking them on the trips that you promised me. Do you really think that I was okay with your relationship with Keisha all these years?"

She paused for a moment to gather herself, and for things to sink in for him, before going on. "The lies, the women, I mean, did you honestly think that I would be here forever while you walked on me? You put me and your son in jeopardy without thinking, Ace. I stuck around as long as I could and I do love you, but Brother, I don't love you that much. For the first time in my life, I'm happy and I feel appreciated. If you love me like you claim you do, then please respect my decision to move on."

She was ecstatic that she was finally able to take the load that he had placed on her heart, and give it back to him. She came to the guilt-free conclusion that had she known how happy she would be having left him, she would have done it a long time ago.

Ace, however, sat there for a second. With an eerily speechlessness, he finally manned up. "Yeah, whatever. Tell my son I'll pick him up in the afternoon for the celebrity basketball game." He pulled off leaving Samira in the middle of the street having never looked her directly in the eye. He rolled out feeling crushed and remembering her words that held such truth behind them. At one time he had tried to beat it out of her. "I'ma find someone else to love me and your son." He realized, 'time waits for no one' was way more than a catchy phrase.

*God stopped the world and took a piece of rib to make me*

*I am the Mother of civilization,*

*I give birth to nations*

*Powerful as she may be,*

*Does she really know who she is?*

*Letting your body be used for a post for niggas who don't*

*deserve it*

*I mean, since we on the topic*

*You are every woman and all the woman he should need*

*So that fake ass player shit,*

*Save it for someone else to believe*

*I did you favor and almost lost my life giving your life*

*A second chance*

*I had your baby,*

*Now I know that sounds crazy*

*But instead of fixing your lips to call me a bitch*

*You need to be thinking of a way to repay me*


## WHAT AM I REALLY WORTH?

It was a nice day in the hood, and the streets were packed. The car show was in full swing. The Lost Boys had it right. There were Jeeps, Lex' coupes, Beamers and Benzes, for days. It was as though the whole city was in Prices Park. It was crazy. Ace could barely get to his mother's house with the traffic moving so slowly. As he inched towards home, he watched the girls walking by half dressed, crazy wig weaves and long ponytails. *The boy, Little UC is doin' big things*, he thought, peeping the festivities. He watched activities for the children, vendors, and banners flying bearing the phrase, 'Welcome Home Hashim Fennell and Shakir Leatherbury' on them. It was unreal.

Minutes later, he parked in front of his mom's and ran in to get dressed for the day. He wanted to scoop up Ali. He threw on a fresh white tee with his jeans rolled up above the ankles like the Akees at the Masjid. With his shiny Rolex and a pair of 'butters' he flew downstairs and headed for the door when his mom called for him.

Ace appeared in the kitchen doorway to see what she wanted. "Samira called and said she would drop little Ali off instead of you picking him up," Mrs. Prince relayed.

Puzzled, he snapped, "Whatever! That girl better stop playin' with me and my son before I snap! When she comes, just have her bring him to the park. I'ma go catch the game!"

His mom sent up a prayer for her child's peace of mind, as she watched him storm out the door.

Embarrassed by going from a '350 Benz to an '88 Honda, he walked the short distance down the block to the park. A chill went through him as he walked past the projects that were now newly renovated townhomes. When he arrived, the first person he spotted was Jasmine with her loud self, on one of those little Ninja bikes.

"Jazz!" he called.

She looked over at him screaming and waving wildly,

"Ace! What up babe?"

He kept it moving, feeling like a total stranger on the scene until he saw Kedar leaning on his squatter. Simone was in the passenger's seat window down, with her ever present Newport poised between her index and middle fingers. Ace and Kedar gave each other some dap then Ace leaned back on the car to view the people.

Music blasted from all angles, and Ace felt a little more in the groove until his eyes rested upon a black Lumina with tinted windows. Little UC and crew popped out, one-by-one, confirming to Ace that their bling had lost none of its shine. The burgundy Jaguar that pulled up behind UC seriously caught his attention as UC waited for the person to get out.

Had Ace's face been concrete, it would have most certainly cracked when he saw Rick get out of the car. The two men walked down the hill to the court together, with much conversation between the two of them. They turned to look at Ace.

Neither party uttered a word. They just stared.

"Damn, go give him a hug," urged Simone, who was eyeing Ace eyeing Rick. "You and him still ain't speakin'? Damn-y'all worse than bitches!"

"Shut the fuck up!" yelled Kedar hoping Ace wouldn't respond to her madness. Then he pushed Ace to get his attention. Walking towards them was Nikki and the baby. Ace didn't want to play himself, so he didn't say anything. She was fussing over the baby and talking on her cell phone, so she didn't even notice them. Internally beside himself, Ace just peeped the whole scene, observing how the tables had turned. He was gone less than two years, and niggas who weren't getting it before, were now on top; it was like everybody forgot who the hell he was.

Simone and Kedar got out of the car, and started towards the basketball court because tip-off was about to be under way. Ace simply leaned back on the car, stuck and confused. His thoughts were broken by, "Ace-still lookin' good."

He lifted his head to find Cianni, with her fine ass, Cherise and Jew'ell. "You still lookin' good," Cianni repeated.

Trailing behind Cianni was her shadow, Akil, a little rowdy nigga she called her brother.

"Aw nigga, you ain't do no real time," said Akil stepping to Ace. " Luckily you just got out nigga, or you would be my next victim. But your boy, Rick, flossin' through the city real lovely."

The infamous smirk returned to his lips as he checked Akil's tattoos. One gun on each arm; he couldn't help thinking that he should have had him on his team.

"Yeah well that ain't my boy, but everybody gets a chance to be king at least once," said Ace genuinely tickled by the young boy's fire.

"Well you know kings can be dethroned," Akil giggled quietly yet sneakily.

"Ak, shut up! Let's just go watch the game," said Cianni, sick of hearing him talk shit.

He shook himself out of the trance that he had sunken back into and strolled towards the courts. Haji spotted him as soon as he got to the fence, and moved through the crowd to greet him.

"Ace, what up man?" he said hugging his life-long friend.

"Yo!" said Ace touched by Hashim's show of unconditional love. "Haji, you never got caught up in the things we got into, now all the hard work has paid off. You made it. That's what's up!" Ace said with hearty, honest praise.

Hashim responded, "Man, hustlin' don't pay. It's just a temporary satisfaction. The bonus is jail and the risk, well you know the risk. It ain't no rules. No one is exempt. People's lives get lost either by buying your product, or by getting killed by your slip-ups. Anyway, just stay man, I'll catch you after the game." Ace found a seat on the bleachers.

## The Lies Hustlers Never Tell

As he watched the game and the people, Hashim's words bounced around in his head similar to the dribbling ball that had spared him his life.

*Shahida T. Fennell*

*From the 60's to the 70's*
*To the 80's and the 90's*
*Now the new millennium, seems far too exciting*
*Different drug of choice,*
*Different hustler's voice*
*Same corner, just a new face that serves you*
*Instead of her,*
*Now it's her daughter that thinks she's a dime piece*
*And the police*
*It's that same cracker from school*
*You punched in the face, you got to face*
*The gear is still the same*
*Just a new designer*
*And money went from small to big faces*
*Instead of low-riders,*
*Its Benzes that they chasing*
*And the junkie you serving,*
*Well, you just switched places*
*'Cause he was the man then,*
*And you the man now*
*The game don't change*
*It just goes in a circle, sort of like a merry-go-round*
*The game don't change just the players*
*Same block, different name*
*Same product, different slang,*

## THE GAME DON'T CHANGE

# ACKNOWLEDGEMENTS

*First thank the Creator. There is only one God and his name is Allah. Hashim, Nadirah, Weusi, and Ali my reason for breathing and striving.*

*For helping financially it has been a long journey. And I do appreciate everyones sincere help, those that have left the struggle, you are well appreciated Julienne Fennell, Raye Avery (if every teacher were like you all children would succeed), Vernell and Joyce Proctor (Big Uncle and the Diva), Aunt Ilene and Levi Williams (Auntie, thanks for the special talks and encouragement), Kendall (KB) Briscoe (you made the idea possible, good looking), Bryant and Wiggles Allenye (Bee friends for life), Rob Redden-Hutt (that ain't double RR on the cover, is it), Roger (Akee) Gordon (thanks for believing in me till the end - you are the meaning of a good Muslim brother), James Freeman (little things mean a lot), Nikki Hackett (helping to support the struggle in more ways than one), Zulema Golston (being there when needed the most in ways you wouldn't image), Angel Richardson (marketing is everything and you did a good job), Jenaye Fennell (no matter what goes on, you always seem to be there for me at the right time and I love you for that), Hanifa and Haneef (thanks for being there thru all of my idea's from the smallest one to the biggest. Much support)*

*Special thanks to* **ERIC (Eekerbeek) Johnson**----*thanks for being there in the clutch 12 years+4 ever is all that can describe the bond we have (no way out) Love you*

*(SISTERS)--------------***April Fennell, Jewel Sanchez**
*(the beginning of a life time) Meeka Speight, Savette, Chonda Frazier, Jennifer Sweeney, Tish Smoke, Shaylynn Flonnery, Monique Davis (Moe Moe), Tiara and Taylor Proctor*

*(My real brother)-----**Damon Nelson** true brother till the end there are no words to describe what you mean to me, no matter up or down, you got my back, smoke clears and there's no one you always seem to come thru regardless from getting money to being broke, thru tears to laughter seems no matter what happens you stay in the shadow I'll always love my big brother Duck*

*(Close friends)-----------Connie Robinson, Sharmeka Thompson, Sadie and Quinn Thomas, Tyrea Rollins (Sly TY), Ebony Stewart (your the only one to keep it real from the hill top days till the end, my friend, a dime plus), Tammy Bowen*
*(Brothers)------------Shawn (Jihad) Kelly, Kwigs, Jermiah, Abdullah McKnight, Lewis Ames, Jordan McBoob, Malik Johnson (one of the realist bars don't lock forever), Brian Camille (good looking out), Repo (the hood santa), Shy the skinny pimp, Kenneth Coleman, Little Kevin, Steve, Willy Brothers, Kevin (Nafie) White (my brother when you want wanna be), Damon Wilson, Michael (Scooby) Eddie Frazier.*

*FAMILY*
*(Muslim sisters)------------, Jasmine (Jazzy) Hackett, Karin Cooke (Little Sister KC), Sabiyah Redden, Kimyatta, Trina Mallory, Inez, Wilmore, Nicole Helm, Shantell Prichett, Umm Zaid, Lovey, Gloria, Jahan, Zakia (designing my hijabs), Habeeba (designing my hijabs), Aisha, Gina, Karen (lacing my hair), Ann Wright*
*(Fennells) ------------Ruth and James Fennell, **Zulema Golston Clark (the ride or die friend)**, Jean Knox and family, Ruth Dillard, Aaron and wife Leslie, Little Aaron, Kyle Thomas, Paul (Peanut) Howell Peanut (on lock down) and his real wife Kim, Jenaye, Jihay (the princess), Nicola, Sharmaine Cox, Shira Rosyter, Jay Wright, Tish Ericka Aunt Linda, Anitr Demby,*

William Barbara, Uncle Speedy, Uncle Chris, the whole Howell
family (too many to name all),
(Proctors)-------------Dolores and Vernell, Anthony and
Mrs.Tracey, Aunt Ilene, Uncle Levi, Aunt Freda Smith, Tray,
Bobbie, Dannyell, Kenny, Aunt Phyllis, Arian, Marla, Meeka,
and Black Vice, Richard Blue, Shannon , Aunt Fay, Aunt Doll,
Kermit , Toren and Teresa Oliver,
(Butchers)------**January holding Harlem down**, Aunt Lizzy,
Uncle Phillip, Sam, Johnathan (Rip), Little Phillip, Aunt
Olivia, Little Irvin, and Joey, Michael Bartley, Aunt Gayle.
(Gordons)-----Sylvester and Sharon Gordon, Donald and
Stacey.
(Shabazz)--------Haneef and Hanifa, Adrena
(Johnsons)------Mom Kathy and Rakia
(Redden)----------Tacurra, Darrly, David, Fresh, Kim, Sime,
Orin, Dee, Robin
(McKnights)--------Mom Val, Aunt Della, Meena, Gabriel
(Baby Boog) Little Munch, and Malik, Rick (keep cutting)
mann mann, omar, pete rock (always nigga, nothing in life is
constant but change)
(Flonnory)-------Aunt Phyllis (always there for me, thanks),
God Mom Ann, Mom Mattie, Aunt Dorthea, Trail, Kusha,
Jakeen, Aunt Joyce, Anisa (Golston), Rodney (NYC), Quinton,
Malik, Mom Val, Japal (NYC), Aunt Diann (NYC)
Extra special thanks to all those who were there from the
ambrosia open mic's to the Kinko style books)

**Scrub a dub** (Spice, Rick and Paul), Cliff Henry, Blue Chip,
Talib Salaam, Kito, Aps photo, D-Hover, Skr studios, Dat Baw
Dave, twin poets, Cherise (pretty you), Jerome J-Rock Perkins,
Dee D-Block (nyc), Cousin Gert (coming thru in the clutch),
Chi, Artie Keen Black, Base (Flatline Records), Young Cannon,
Streets, Bryant and Bruce, Totis, Shaneeka Stewart, Rissy,

*Corey Curtis, Manny, Andre (Gator) Henry, Manuel, Fuquan, Wendall (Duce), Turtle (Sweets), Naughty, speak to me (Boo Monie, Jamel and the whole Crew), Stevie Nixon, Big Oak, Night Crew at work (Leon I mean Bob, Mrs Carmen, KO, Moon, Mrs Charlotte, Angel), Will Camp, Mr Michael Johnson (greatest Grandpop award), Medina, Mike Brown and Moshay (where ever you are in Philly), Tanya Johnson, Little Bobbie (east), Little and Big Nugget, Vincent (69) Wilson, Idris, Stink( Hilltop), Cub, Ranessha (Chester), Saud Clark (Philly), Biz (Team PB), Patrice Clark (Philly), Lips, Maul, and Elie for looking out when the doors were closed, T-Dot (Terrence),Uncle Tom White, (Aunt Rhonda, Mee-Mee, George, Myisha), Jaws (South), Mar, Dre Polk (DP), Breakout (Ty and your wife for your support) D.O.C. (thanks for the ride), Sheena.*

**To all those on lock down who are sometimes forgotten** ---
*Kevin (Saleem) Black, Skippy, Block, Moe Good, Jafist, Odb, Ronaldo (20 Money), Strecth (stick with them dimes), Michael Bartley (love you cousin), Coley Hobson, Michael Righter, Arthur Baker, Yahim, Latan, Javon (Southbridge Trooper), D-Hover (blessed), key (love you cousin), Jambo (Pretty Nigga Hilltop), Bruce Stewart, Jerry (Poison) Williams, Butter, Shawn McQuary, Bee, Wolfee*

**To all the fallen soldiers who lost their lives in this struggle**
*Damon Emory (we haven't forgotten about you George), Kenny Davis, Marty, Arthur Wells (Love You Babe) Little Howard, Wali,*

*Special Thanks From The Editor:*

*There are many I have forgotten but much respect and love*

*Thank you for your special contributions:*
*Skip, Joe and Courtney (Philly)*
*E-Double, Miles Cooley, Craig Jennifer Bryant, Brian Green,*
*Deke, Paris Payton, Michelle Burgee, The Enigma Poets (Chi-*
*town) Bernard Jenkins, Nykole Goodwine, Michelle DeVillers,*
*Doris Moody, Joyce Jones, Victor Porter, Christopher Williams*
*and the entire Pre Paid Legal Services family esp. Team Nu*
*Vision and Dallas, "The Only Chip On The Cookie!"*
*Kharisma Boyer, Warrick and Takicha Roundtree and the*
*Untamed Tongues Family and Jorai (Las Vegas)*
*Speak to me*
*Chuck and the Charlie B's Family.*

**COMING SOON!!!**

# THE
# TRUTH
# ABOUT
# CIANNI

## by Shahida T. Fennell

Cianni, the typical long haired light skin girl, body built like a coke bottle; you know, slim where needed and fat in places they all notice. Cianni gets in her light blue CI645 BMW driving away from her apartment she shares with her younger sister Je-Well. She puts on her theme song by Destiny's Child, Ti and 'Lil Wayne "I need a Soldier"--

"If your status ain't hood
I ain't checkin' for him
Betta be street if he lookin' at me
I need a soldier

Before reaching the prison Cianni stops off on 2- 4 (also known as 24th street) to get some Dro (weed). "It's on now! My peoples is home," she thought as she drove to Howard Young Correctional Facility to pick up Akil while bumpin' her music.

Nose turned up as she looked at her missed calls "DAMN! Shawn called like six times! That nigga be buggin'! she thought to herself as she pulled up in front of the prison. The glass to the prison was tinted so she couldn't see if he was up front or not. As she adjusted her mirror to make sure she was looking scrumptious, she put on some more MAC lip gloss and turned the music down.

Just a little startled by the tap on the window, her face gleamed as she looked up to see this brown skinned, brown eyes medium build brother. His hair pulled back in a pony tail with his D.O.C. all whitesd on. She pops the lock as he peeks in the car.

"CeeCee" he calls her for short, "wait!"

She says, "Let me give you a hug!"

She gets out of the car, struts around to the passenger side and gives him a big hug. As she does, she can hear sounds coming from the windows of the prison of people yelling and banging on the window.

"You still sexy brother!" She says as she hugs him tightly.

"Yeah! You know jail preserves a nigga" he replied as they both enter the car.

"Yo! Look on the back seat, I got some gear for you. You hungry?" she asked

"Hell yeah, you know jailhouse food ain't the look" as his stomach growled from the smell.

"Let me stop at Mrs. Lee's to get a dutch." she said before she pulled the dro out of her Gucci clutch pocket book. Akil eyeing her every movement

"Cee you know I'm hungry let's hit KFC (Kentucky Fried Chicken) and it's for more than just food," as his eyes stayed on CiannI's legs, which were half showing through the red wrap around dress accented by her red and blue Gucci sneaker.

"You still rolling big like always" says Akil as they pull off into the parking lot of KFC.

"You like my new Gucci sneaks?" she asked seductivly.

"I know how you roll big things. You lookin' real sexy Cee Cee." Akil replied.

She gave him a look that could make the D.O.C.'s fall right off.

# A Nu Direction Publishing

## A Division of MeJah Books Inc.
## ORDER FORM

MeJah Books Inc.
333 Naamans Road
Tri-State Mall #12-13
Claymont, DE 19703
(302)793-3424

---

### Purchaser Information

Name:_____

SBI#_____(if applicable)

Address:_____Apt#_____

City:_____ State:_____ Zip Code:_____

---

Please Specify Quanity Below:

| | | |
|---|---|---|
| The Lies Hustlers Never Tell | _____ | @$14.95=_____ |
| T-Shirt | _____ | @$12.00=_____ |
| Poems On Cd | _____ | @$10.00=_____ |

Shipping & Handling (via U.S. Media Mail)...............................$3.00
*Add $1.00 to postage for each additional purchase*
*Shipping and handling to prisons/institutions.........................FREE*

Total...$_____

**Please make cashier checks and money orders payable to**
MeJah Books Inc.

Forms of payments accepted: Credit Cards, Cashier Checks and Money Orders

---

### Credit Card Payment Form

**Cardholder's Full Name:**_____

**Address:**_____

**City:**_____**State:**_____**Zip:**_____

**Card Number**_____

**Signature:**_____**Exp Date:___/___**

**Phone:**_____ ☐ *Visa/Mastercard*

**Email:**_____ ☐ *Discover*

☐ *AmericanExpress*

I'd like to hear what you thought about my first work of fiction.
Feel free to write.

Shahida T. Fennell
P.O Box 1421
Wilmington, DE 19899

Email: shahida8774@yahoo.com